JAMES P. BLAYLOCK

*This special signed edition
is limited to
1000 numbered copies.*

This is copy __878__.

River's Edge

James P. Blaylock

Illustrated by J. K. Potter

Subterranean Press 2017

First Edition

ISBN
978-1-59606-838-4

Subterranean Press
PO Box 190106
Burton, MI 48519

subterraneanpress.com

For
Paul Buchanan, friend, fellow writer and teacher, breakfast companion, and early reader of my books and stories. Cheers!

Acknowledgements

I'M GRATEFUL, AS EVER, for the help of my wife Viki, who tirelessly reads my manuscripts, ever on the lookout for misspellings, bad sentences, plot errors, and other literary embarrassments. And also to my friend and agent John Berlyne, who reads them with an eye toward sweeping away base Americanisms and misunderstandings and keeping me on the correct side of the river. Any errors in this book I claim as my own.

"Imagination is the real and eternal world of which this vegetable universe is but a faint shadow."

—William Blake

Chapter 1

Kent, England,
Along the River Medway

L ANGDON ST. IVES AND his friend Hasbro stood in the darkness some few feet from Eccles Brook behind the Majestic Paper Mill. The brook was fifteen feet wide and moderately deep, and it flowed another two hundred yards at an easy descent before emptying into the Medway. There was half a moon in the sky, but the two men were hidden in the shadows of immense oaks with solid, leafy canopies. A beech forest stretched away behind, the filtered moonlight stippling the trunks white, and a breeze cast moving shadows among the trees.

The two men whom St. Ives had seen a few minutes ago had disappeared, back into the mill, or so St. Ives hoped. Although he carried his shillelagh, and could fight with it if he was pressed, fighting wasn't sensible unless they were attacked. He had no desire to knock anyone on the head, especially watchmen from the mill who were simply doing their duty. He and Hasbro were not trespassing, but they were snooping, engaged on a mission that St. Ives intended to keep secret until he was certain he understood the meaning of their discoveries.

They moved out from behind the trunk of the oak now and made their way down to the bank again. In his knapsack, St. Ives carried half a dozen leather-covered flasks, five of which they had already filled with water from various parts of the brook. The water stank badly of lye and bleach and other noxious chemicals, and in the brook it ran dirty-white with a brown froth. Twelve hours ago, at midday, it had been moderately clear—not clean, but the effluent from a paper mill could scarcely be made clean. Hasbro dipped a pint of foamy water from an eddy and poured it carefully into a flask, closing the stopper. St. Ives took it from him and slipped it into the knapsack.

They walked farther along the brook-side path, St. Ives pointing out a dead fish entangled in waterweeds. He handed his shillelagh to Hasbro and stepped down onto a convenient rock in order to net the fish. It was a common chub, but it took him a moment to be certain of it, because the body was badly misshapen from ruptured cancers in the flesh. Its mouth was open wide and its eyes were a furry white. He laid it onto a piece of parchment paper that he folded carefully around it before putting it into the knapsack along with the water samples. There were already twenty or so poisoned fish preserved at home and another dozen that Dr. Pullman, the local coroner, was dissecting in his laboratory. Dr. Pullman was a chemist as well as an anatomist. Like St. Ives, he much preferred a live fish to a dead fish, unless the creature was frying in a pan.

The dead chub wasn't apparently different from the others that St. Ives and Hasbro had collected except in species, there being bream, carp, pike and eels among the corpses he had netted from the Medway, all with the telltale cancers. And there were hundreds of the poisoned fishes washing ashore at low tide along the Wouldham Marshes downriver, along with a half dozen species of dead water birds.

St. Ives realized that he had strayed into a patch of moonlight, and he stepped back into the shadows at the same moment that he heard a low whistle and then the crack of a stick breaking nearby. Hasbro turned at the sound of it, raising the shillelagh. A short, broad-shouldered man rushed at him, holding a length of iron pipe that was drawn back in his upraised hand. Hasbro whipped the shillelagh around in a tight arc just as the man was upon him, hitting his wrist and knocking the pipe aside, and then swinging the shillelagh underhanded and slamming it upward between his legs.

The man pitched to the ground, shouting the name "Davis!" aloud. There was the sound of groaning and of running feet, and Davis, a tall, lanky man with a long face and wearing a tweed cap, appeared some twenty yards away, heading at them hell-bent down the moon-lit path. St. Ives and Hasbro bolted in the direction of the beech woods, running hard toward the east along a half-overgrown track, not slowing down until they were a quarter of a mile removed from the environs of the mill. St. Ives looked back and saw no one following, and they went on at an easier pace.

Very shortly they turned down a familiar path, crossing Eccles Brook a mile upstream, where the water ran clear and clean. The path forked, the left hand angling away northeast to Kit's Coty House, the Neolithic long barrow above the village of Eccles with its ancient standing stones. They turned southwest toward Aylesford, where the path emerged at the top of the weir near the stone bridge. Their foray tonight marked the end of their investigation into the secrets of the Majestic Paper Mill, which had clearly been damming up effluents during the day, and flushing them into the River Medway in the dead of night.

Chapter 2

The Majestic Paper Mill

JUST THE ONE WORD, 'strike,'" Henley Townover said to his father. "It was chalked on the east door beneath a handbill that advised employees to report troubling issues to the London Trades Council with a halfpenny postcard. Davis found it this morning."

Henley and Charles Townover stood in the offices that were elevated high above the floor of the Majestic Paper Mill in Snodland. Through a broad window they looked down on a room filled with Hollander beaters, the chopped cotton rags within the beaters disintegrating in a heavy solution of caustic lye. The mill workers were girls and were referred to as Paper Dolls in Snodland across the river and in the nearby villages. They moved among the troughs and machinery ten hours a day, wearing jaunty paper hats, newly folded each morning and noonday. They also wore gloves and goggles against the chemical mixtures churning within the beaters and proofing in the dye pots.

"Davis eradicated it before the girls arrived?" Charles Townover asked. He was an old man, getting on toward seventy, although still apparently hale. He rubbed his hands in a circular motion now, as if he were washing them.

"Some must have seen it, Father," Henley said. "It's possible that the chalk mark was the work of one of the girls."

"*Chalk*," Charles Townover said with evident disgust, "a weak-willed, cowardly, ungrateful effort, and ineffective into the bargain. If a person is going to make threats, he had best shout them out loud when people are bound to hear. This shameful, sneaking timidity compounds the crime. Who do we believe posted the handbill?"

"Davis observed a man talking to three of the girls yesterday evening along the footpath—a union man, he said. He was carrying what must have been a number of the handbills, no doubt distributing them to the girls."

"Davis was *certain* of this union man?"

"Tolerably so."

Charles Townover shook his head. "It was inevitable, I suppose, given the success of the mill. These unions are like flies to honey, scattering their filthy liberal notions. But we shall deal with the man in our own way if we see him again."

The old man fell silent now, evidently considering what he had learned. He looked out at the view of the River Medway and the village of Snodland on the opposite shore. The mill, which produced good rag paper, both linen and cotton, had moved into the present quarters after months of renovation and construction. They had shifted out of London to this more idyllic location along the river, and to provide some distance from the baleful eye of the scalawag William Gladstone's government, which elevated the worker at the expense of the Crown and the common interest. Liberals, he thought, would be improved by being taken out and flogged. "The safety of the girls is paramount, of course. I mean to keep them from doing themselves a mischief. They're young, and they haven't enough perspicacity between them to see through a pair of spectacles. Summon Davis, if you will, Henley."

Davis, the mill foreman, was a lean, ropy, red-haired man with a wandering left eye and bad teeth. He wore an old tweed cap, sweat-stained, which Charles Townover found crude and offensive. But the man did his work, and his cap was his own business. Davis stood now on the catwalk beyond the glass, looking down onto the mill floor through a pair of binoculars in order to bring the far corners into view. Skylights illuminated the enormous rooms, along with several hundred coal-oil lamps, hooded to inhibit the dispersal of coal dust from the burnt oil, which might soil the paper pulp if it found its way into the vats. Henley rapped against the glass, and Davis turned, nodded at Henley's gesture, surreptitiously returned Henley's wink, and entered the offices through a swinging door.

"Mr. Davis, tell me about this man you observed speaking to the three Paper Dolls," Townover said.

"A union man, I don't doubt. One of the girls—I don't like to say, but it was Daisy Dumpel, sir—she was giving him an earful of her swollen throat and the croup and the quinsy. She was poisoned by the chemicals, she said—the same old story again. I stood in the shadows and heard enough of their talk to be sure of it. Then the other two girls went away, like they didn't want to be a part of this, and when they were gone, the man put his hands on Daisy. I nearly stepped out and put paid to his caper, but Daisy didn't seem to take offense, and so I hung back to see whether the man would commit himself to a crime."

"Put his *hands* on her? Do you mean to say that the man is a common ravisher as well as a union lackey?"

"There's hell-hounds in every profession, sir, and she's a pretty thing, in her way, and seemed willing."

Through the window, Townover caught sight of a carriage turning up from the River Road, an elegant coach and four that certainly belonged to Gilbert Frobisher, a preposterously rich man, retired from business, who had a taste for fine paper. Frobisher was one of three potential investors touring the mill this very morning. The coach passed out of sight beneath the trees. "Do you believe this union man to be one of the men whom you discovered lurking along the creek four nights back, the two that set upon Jenks?"

"Sure, it might have been. The shadows were deep, though, and they broke and ran before I got a good look."

Townover nodded and said, "If this union man sets foot in the vicinity again I want you and Jenks to provide him with a proper thrashing. Meanwhile, Davis, alert the constable that the man was seen molesting one of our Paper Dolls. You needn't mention the chalked slogan or the handbills. I have no desire to imply that there are troubles here at the Majestic. I simply want the man... educated."

"I understand completely, sir."

"As for Daisy Dumpel, the girl is too frail for real work. We'll send her home before she makes trouble. See to it, Henley. Give the girl a generous sum—one hundred pounds. That should be enough to make her quite happy. Make it a bank cheque with a note of provenance.

We don't want her robbed. She's to negotiate it on Threadneedle Street, at the bank itself, so put her on the train to London without delay. Who was with Daisy?— the other two girls?"

"The girl Clo. Clover Cantwell," Davis said, "and Nancy Bates."

"Clover's name is familiar to me, but I cannot recall why."

"You'll remember," Henley told him, "that the girl has an aged aunt in Maidstone, the old dowager who attended the soirée when we opened our doors to business, quite down on her luck at present. It was she who requested that we give her niece employment."

"Yes, of course. The girl had been in some trouble in London, I believe."

"She was taken up for petty theft, but was shown leniency—the intervention of the dowager aunt again."

"Good. The girl is in a tenuous position. She'll be biddable, I believe."

"Surely she would be grateful if we did her aunt a service of some sort, a small show of generosity. We might profit from having a willing agent among the girls, so to speak."

"Excellent notion," Townover said. "Call Miss Cantwell upstairs, Davis. And the instant that Daisy Dumpel is put aboard the London train and difficult to recall, report this union man's outrageous behavior to the constable, along with the sad fact that Daisy chose to return to her parents' home, no doubt in fear of her safety at the hands of this fiend."

"Yes, sir."

"And one more thing, Davis. Is all in train in the lobby? The Paper Dolls are dressed suitably, paper and paint at the ready, refreshments at hand? The prettiest of the Dolls is to see to Mr. Frobisher. Not too slight of figure, if you take my meaning."

"They've been ready this past half-hour. The Archer girl with the blond ringlets will see to Mr. Frobisher."

Davis left the office and moved downstairs toward the deckle room, where frames containing wet slurries of paper were coming out of the vats. When he was well out of earshot, Townover said to Henley, "It grieves me to think that it was one of the girls who scrawled the message in chalk. It's simply ungrateful. I don't like it at all."

"A percentage of the population is born ungrateful," Henley said.

"You're in the right of it, unfortunately. Too many bad apples these days. Why don't they come to *me*, though? If it's a matter of wages, we can find them another shilling or two. I'm not an unreasonable man. Discover what you can from Miss Cantwell."

"I believe that we can learn a great deal with the encouragement of a ten-pound note."

"Which will never see the inside of her poor aunt's purse. This is exactly my point, Henley. In my day people were encouraged to do the right thing because it was the right thing to do, not because they smelled a ten-pound note."

"Times change, Father. Loyalty has fallen out of fashion. Bank notes will never fall out of fashion, I assure you."

Chapter 3

The Paper Dolls

O N THE FLOOR OF the mill, Clover Cantwell immersed an empty, wood-framed deckle into the slurry in the rectangular vat in front of her. She dipped out a porridge of wet paper pulp, which at once began to settle on the tightly woven wire mesh within the deckle frame, the liquid leaking through the mesh and back into the vat. There was a rising cloud of stink from the mixture of bleach and lye, although she scarcely noted it any more—a bad thing, maybe, since the chemical reek was rumored to poison the senses. She wore goggles over her eyes, and heavy india-rubber gloves and apron, and yet after six months of working the deckle she was all too familiar with chemical burns.

She shook and shifted the deckle, draining off the remaining liquid and settling the pulp evenly over the bottom, and then handed it off to the coucher—Elspeth today—who turned the wet paper out onto a felt blanket and covered the paper with yet another blanket to keep it damp until it could be placed in the watermark press. She handed the empty deckle to the runner, the girl who waited on the vat-men, although there were no men among the Paper Dolls, only girls, who were called vat-men out of long tradition. Clover was sick of the stinking slurries in the vats, although the job was better than her first position, tending the oven that roasted bones for the making of bone-brown pigment. Nothing stank worse than burning bone, not even bleach and lye.

Breathing in the stench from the vats would make you sick—she had seen it often enough: the hoarse voice and scalded throat, the blisters on your hands that turned to open sores, and after a time, hair falling out in clumps. The gloves and mask couldn't keep it all out. The dye-making was worse, though. Her friend Mabel had lost her fingernails. Mr. Davis was supposed to move you along before such things happened, but that was just happy-talk. Mr. Davis moved you along when it suited him.

With any luck, Clover would be given a step soon and allowed to work the watermark press, as had happened to Daisy when she got sick, except that Daisy got worse in spite of being shifted from the deckles. Clover amended her definition of luck as she dipped another deckle into the vat: with any luck she would find a rich man to marry, and the mill could cram itself up its own fundament.

She had gone visiting to her aunt's house yesterday morning, Sunday being her free day. Her aunt's house lay in Maidstone, an hour's walk from the Chequers Inn, in Aylesford, where Clover currently lived with Daisy Dumpel. Her aunt was as doddering as her falling-down house. It was an easy thing for Clover to nick the odd few coins or even a banknote from the old lady's purse. There were pieces of silver in the house, too—plate and cutlery and candlesticks and a set of tankards with a crest on them, but Clover had no idea how to profit from them in the local villages. London had been simple in that regard, given that no one looked at a person twice, especially if there was a profit to be made. She had stolen two pounds, three shillings and four pence from her aunt, who squirreled away coins and small banknotes in drawers and pots and jars, as often as not forgetting where. The take amounted to something more than two month's wages at the mill, and would pay the reckoning at the inn, supper included, for some time, and she could forego the tiresome visits to her aunt.

"Clo!" Elspeth said to her. She nodded in the direction of the stairs and took the deckle from Clover without another word. Clover saw that Mr. Davis was jerking his thumb at her. Henley Townover stood inside the office above, looking down on them, and Clover shook her gloves off and called to the runner to take her place. She wondered whether this summons would lead to a bit of luck, or to its opposite.

Henley's father was as rich as the Bank of England, which would make Henley as rich as the Bank of England when the old man died. Clover rather fancied Henley, although he had a hard mouth and was said to be a churchgoing man. Among the Paper Dolls, there were rumors that Henley had been involved in scandal in the months before he had left London to follow his father to Snodland and take his place in the mill. Clover didn't care a fig for churchgoing men, with their prating about virtue and their holier-than-thou airs. It was true, however, that such men had more to lose when they were caught sinning. And there were things about Henley that made her think he would not be averse to sinning. Perhaps, she thought, he and his money might be coerced into sinning with her.

She bowed respectfully when she walked into the office, where Henley sat at his desk now.

"Shut the door, girl," Henley said to her.

Chapter 4

The Investor

G ILBERT FROBISHER CLIMBED down from his coach, all eighteen stone of him landing heavily on the ground. A small, black-haired girl of eight or ten years and with freckled cheeks looked out through the open carriage window unhappily. "I *must* come along with you, Uncle," she said, "else you'll be fleeced like a sheep."

"My instincts are sharp where money is concerned, as you very well know, Larkin. I mean to get the lay of the land without committing myself to a half-farthing. I purposely left my cheque-book in the coach, there in the black case, so keep a weather eye on it." He looked up at the coachman and said, "Take a glass of something to drink and a bite to eat if it's offered to you, Boggs, but I won't be above an hour, for we're due at the St. Ives's for supper."

"May I take a glass, also?" Larkin asked him.

"Barley water, my dear, or lemonade if they offer it. Do you hear that, Boggs? Larkin mustn't drink ale or shrub or anything of the kind."

"Ten-water grog, Uncle?" Larkin asked. "Just a glass of it."

"Not a drop, child. Rum is terrible, pernicious stuff."

Larkin was Gilbert's adopted daughter, whom he'd rescued from a life of crime on the London streets. She had evidently been gallows-bound, being the chief of a piratical gang of children that ran wild along the river. She had gone some way toward saving his life, however, quite literally, when he had been poisoned with a dose of narcotic powders made of pulverized glass eels and non-descript chemicals. Gilbert had come near as a toucher to succumbing to what the newspapers referred to as the "Sargasso Sea lunacy."

At well under six feet tall, Gilbert was the polar oppo-site of Boggs in appearance—Gilbert being very nearly round, whereas Boggs was as tall and thin as a mortician and in fact had something of the appearance of a cadaver, which belied his stamina and his abilities as a coachman. He was a rare hand with a whip, which he used solely as an instrument of speech, flicking it very near the horse's ear but never touching the beast, and carrying on a more detailed conversation by way of whistles and loud clicks of his tongue. He had taught Larkin to drive the horses, and she was a surprisingly quick study, although she was too hellfire rash for her own good.

A sprightly looking, full-figured girl in a clean white paper cap and apron appeared from the mill entrance, made a very pretty bow, and skipped toward them, smiling cheerfully and inviting Gilbert into the entrance hall.

"I'm happy to accompany you, my dear," he said. She reminded him somewhat of his own lost love— Miss Bracken—whom he had last seen fleeing away into an underground cavern, hand in hand with a dwarf. Miss Bracken had quite broken his heart. This girl was younger, much younger. Still the resemblance cheered him. "What is your name, lass?"

"Samantha, sir. You're welcome to call me Sam."

"Sam it is, then. How old might you be?"

"Eighteen years, sir, coming on nineteen. I've been at the mill the past two." She glanced up at Larkin and smiled, although she received no smile in return. "I've never seen a carriage half as magnificent as this, not in all my life," she said, attending to Gilbert again. "Is that your crest on the side, sir? What is that creature that's chewing on the Devil? A hairy dragon, perhaps?"

"A very ferocious hedge-pig, Sam. And those are my initials in gold foil. Gilbert Frobisher at your service." He smiled broadly at her.

"She's fourteen years old, and not a day older, Uncle," Larkin said loudly, giving them both a hard look through the window. "She means to *set the hook*. Don't be a silly fish. Do you hear me now? It was you who told me of the fool and his money."

Sam smiled brightly at Larkin. "Whatever does the girl mean, sir?" she asked Gilbert in a subdued voice. "What *hook?*"

"Larkin natters on in her strange way, dear. Pay no attention."

"I asked do you *hear* me, Uncle? Do you take my meaning or shall I rat you out to Tubby?" Tubby Frobisher was Gilbert's nephew, twenty-five years younger, but the old man's spitting image. Tubby hadn't been fond of Miss Bracken, or of his hapless Uncle's enthusiasms.

"Your meaning is perfectly clear, Larkin, and perfectly unnecessary."

Sam smiled pertly at Larkin, who shook her head slowly, and then ran her finger across her throat. Sam turned away, her smile having evaporated on the instant. She brightened up again, as if by an act of will, and took Gilbert's proffered arm. Already Boggs was turning the horses toward a large carriage-house fifty yards away, and Larkin's window-framed face was dwindling.

Chapter 5

The Open Door

CLOVER HAD NEVER BEFORE been in the offices of the mill, and she looked down from on high now at the Paper Dolls moving about below. Elspeth was working the deckle, and the new girl was stacking paper on the drying racks. She glanced at Henley Townover, who still sat at his desk, writing in a ledger book as if he had forgotten her. He looked up now, however, smiled at her, and asked whether she was happy in her work.

"Yes, sir," she told him. "Quite content."

"Contentment becomes laziness quickly enough, Clover. To what do you aspire, here at the mill? Do you see a future or simply one long-suffering present?"

"Oh, I don't suffer, sir. I'm happy with my lot."

"Come now. Don't play the fool. Surely you've got time to daydream standing at the deckle vats from morning until night. What do you see when you look into the future?"

"Do you mean what do I wish for *sometime*, sir?" She tried reading his face to see what he was about, but he seemed to be neither threatening her nor jesting with her.

"Yes, Clover. Next week, next month, whenever heaven decrees."

"I'd work the watermark press, sir."

"Ah! That's something. Is that the end of it?"

"No, sir, I fancy designing watermarks—making them up." Clover had no aspirations, actually. The idea of remaining at the mill was odious to her.

"You have an artistic flair, then? Like your friend Daisy Dumpel?"

"Some say I do, sir. I don't like to show off, though. My aunt says it's vulgar."

"People often get what they want by showing off, Clover, but there's virtue in humility, certainly. I'd be happy to look at your designs. You're a clever girl, and my father and I believe in helping those who are willing to help us."

"And who help themselves, mayhaps, as they say?" She smiled, regarding him steadily.

Henley favored her with a smile of his own now, looking her up and down as men often did, for reasons that

Clover very much understood. She raised her eyebrows just slightly to put a hint of lasciviousness into her smile, if he chose to read it that way. "Is there some particular *way* in which I can help?"

"There is. I want to ask you about this chalk mark on the door. Surely you've heard of it. I can tell you that Mr. Davis observed three of the girls speaking to a union man. He did not *choose* to name names, but I convinced him that it was for the best, and he named you particularly, Clover, along with Daisy and Nancy Bates."

"I had nothing to say to the union man, and I didn't look at his paper, nor take it neither."

"Good for you. But do you believe that he *was* a union man?"

"Yes. He was asking questions, you know, about the mill. A troublemaker, I said to myself. I could see it straightaway. And then there was the handbill. We were to share it with the others, he said."

"Did he say his name?"

"He said that we might call him Bill Henry but mustn't call him late for supper. It was a joke, do you see, which is why I recall it."

"And did this Bill Henry offer to abuse any of the three of you in any way? My father will not allow that, nor will I."

"I don't take your meaning, sir."

"I believe you do, Clover. Mr. Davis told me that this man laid his hands on Daisy."

"Was Mr. Davis there, sir?"

"Don't play the mooncalf, girl. It doesn't suit you, and it certainly doesn't fool me. Mr. Davis could scarcely have seen what he saw if he was *not* there. I hope you won't attempt to protect this union scrub with an untruth."

"Oh, no, sir," Clover said, looking down at the floor. "Mr. Davis is in the right of it. The man took a fancy to Daisy and put his hand around her shoulder, very friendly like. More than friendly."

"Did he now? And did she take a fancy to *him?* Tell me the truth, Clover. Such a thing is not a crime. Daisy shall not be punished."

"She gave him the glad eye, yes. Later she told me so. We room together at the Chequers, in Aylesford."

"Might Daisy foment trouble for the mill, do you think, consorting with this union fellow? Is she possibly an agitator, I mean to say? Do you understand that word, Clover? An agent, a troublemaker?"

"I heard something like that from Daisy, sir, but surely it's nothing. It don't bear telling."

"Out with it, then. I'll know whether it's something or nothing. It's for the good of Daisy and the good of the mill."

"Well, sir, Daisy's been out to Hereafter Farm, is what she's been telling me. Her sister worked there once, in the scullery."

"Hereafter Farm? I've heard worrisome rumors about that place. Modern, libertine notions. What do you know about it?"

"It's just out from Aylesford Village, sir, back in the woods. Daisy says that the woman there, Mother somebody, has got a society about saving the fish. This Mother woman has taken against industry. They have meetings, and Daisy's gone to them. She told me that she was going again, to a soirée, she called it, with all manner of famous people from London."

Henley Townover put his fingers together and worked them like a spider on a mirror, looking through the window at the river, blue-green in the afternoon sunlight. Clover had told him nothing that he didn't already know except that Daisy had apparently been a turncoat for some time. "I've met your aunt," he said, "the Dowager who lives in Maidstone. She visited the mill some time ago to recommend you for a position. I've wondered how she's getting along."

"Fair, sir, but always one step ahead of the wolf. I help her out with the odd half crown when I can. I gave her my savings last Sunday, two pounds and some shillings."

"Good for you, Clover, but I'm sorry to hear that it's necessary."

"She's desperate poor, sir, but too proud to take help except from me—from family, I mean. There's no family but me."

"She's a respectable woman who has fallen upon unfortunate circumstances. The scriptures tell us that time and chance happen to us all, and to count our blessings. Remind me of her name again."

"Emily, sir. Emily Gower."

"Of course." He opened the desk drawer and removed a square, heavy glass chemist's bottle with a clamped-down lid. The bottle was half full of liquid and sat on a folded piece of cloth. Below the cloth was a leather wallet, from which he took two ten-pound banknotes. It looked to Clover to contain fifty more, and she wondered whether there were larger notes below—twenty pounds, or fifty… "Would you convey our regards to your Aunt Emily along with this gift?" Henley asked. "Twenty pounds might perhaps help her through any present difficulties. If it does not, then surely the two of us can find a means to beget more, so to speak."

"*Beget*, sir—that's another word from the Bible, I believe."

"Indeed it is, Clover."

"Well, sir, my aunt will be uncommonly grateful, as am I." Clover forced herself to weep now—not a difficult trick, since she'd practiced it often enough. She took the proffered banknotes, still thinking of the sheaf of notes left in the wallet. "What's that sir?—in the bottle?" she asked. "My Aunt Gower has such a bottle, the exact same, full of water with Paris green in it, sitting in a window so that it catches the sunlight. It's very like an emerald."

"It's called chloroform, Clover. Have you heard of it?"

"Like chloral? The sleeping potion?"

"Something like. It quietens a frightened girl so that she's more…tractable. Do you understand me?"

"I believe I do, sir. When I was at Miss Sidney's Academy, tractable was what I wasn't. That's what they said when I was sent away."

"I'm not at all surprised," Henley said, and he replaced the cloth and bottle and closed the desk drawer but didn't bother to lock it.

He reached out and grasped Clover's hand, nodding at her thoughtfully. "Keep your eyes and ears open, Clover. Come to see me whenever you have something to say to me—anything at all. Mr. Davis will admit you, although if you'd rather not be seen, wait until the girls have gone along home. My door is always open to you, and our dealings will be perfectly private, if you take my meaning."

"What shall I say *now*, sir?"

"Say that you've been promoted to the watermark press, which is the truth of it."

"What of Daisy?"

"Never you worry about Daisy. She'll be paid off handsomely and is bound for London on the morning train for the sake of her own safety. She means to live with her family. My father is a generous man, you know, and I try to emulate him in that regard. So sketch out your notions for a series of watermarks. I'll have a look at them, although I warn you that we have very high standards, my father and I."

"Thank-you sir," she said, putting the banknotes into her pocket. She curtseyed and walked out through the door, forcing herself to swallow the smile that wanted very badly to appear on her face. She was twenty pounds to the better and free of the deckle vats at last. When she passed Davis on the landing, he touched the brim of his hat, thrust his tongue out at her indecently, and then turned without speaking and ascended the stairs.

Chapter 6

The Message
on the Window

I NSIDE THE MILL, GILBERT Frobisher saw
that the great hall was bright in the sunlight coming
through windows in the roof. The place was strung
with bunting, and there were tables set roundabout with
half a dozen girls in paper hats and aprons, folding multi-
colored sheets of paper into the shapes of swans and paper
boats. He accepted a glass of punch from a girl who wore
a bowtie in the shape of a butterfly, painted realistically
in half a dozen colors.

"Is this the origami, then?" Gilbert asked Samantha.

"Yes, Mr. Frobisher. We're taught the art of paper
folding straightaway. It comes from Japan, which is on

the other side of the world, of all things. What animal do you fancy? We're quite good at birds."

"I'm quite fond of peacocks, although I imagine that it must be difficult to fashion such a creature out of paper. I own a score of peacocks on my property in Dicker, my dear. They perch on the roof moaning like unhappy spirits."

Sam led him to a table occupied by a thin, dark-haired girl in spectacles, perhaps Samantha's age or a year or two older. "Daisy is the only one among us clever enough to fold peacocks," Sam told him, and immediately Daisy began to do just that, selecting a large sheet of tracing paper, her hands folding and creasing rapidly as she turned it this way and that, flipping it over, half dismantling it and then starting out again with counter-folds and fresh creases, clipping bits out with a scissor until she produced a peacock with what appeared to be a full range of feathers as Gilbert watched in fascination. She turned to a palette of watercolor paints now, and without a word she wetted her brush and lapped up the color blue. She worked quickly but with great attention, daubing black along the edge of the blue and then a swathe of green.

Abruptly she stopped, dropped the brush, put her hand over her mouth, and began to cough, her face flushed and twisted with the effort. She gasped for breath now, looking quite pale. Gilbert saw that there was a spray of red across the partly painted tail feathers of the peacock—blood he realized, not paint. Her fit subsided. She regained control over her breathing, wiped her mouth, picked up her brush, and went on with her work.

"Daisy has the megrims so bad sometimes that she believes her head might explode," Sam said to Gilbert, "and a ratchety cough. It's the miasma from the vats as does it…"

She abruptly stopped speaking and looked downward as a voice behind them said, "Mr. Frobisher has no desire to hear about Daisy's croup, Samantha, or for idle gossip of any nature. Keep to your station, if you please."

Gilbert turned to discover Charles Townover with a stormy look about him. His face was brick red, suffused with anger. He removed a flask from his breast pocket and uncorked it, waving it under his nose before swallowing a small draught. He composed himself by an act of will and favored Gilbert with a thin-lipped smile. The two men shook hands. "It's the angina," Townover told him, holding up the flask. "Nitroglycerine, if you can believe it." He thumped his chest with the side of his fist. "Works very quickly, unlike most of the girls, who waste their time at every opportunity. It's no wonder they don't get on in the world."

"Ah," Gilbert said, making an interested face. He hadn't seen Charles Townover for several years, and had known him first at school where he had the reputation of being a prig. The two had been friends, however, and he found himself unsettled by the man's unpleasantness now. He seemed to have undergone some sort of petrifaction as he had grown older.

"And you, Daisy," Townover said, "when you've finished painting Mr. Frobisher's peacock you will report to Mr. Davis and inform him that I've released you from duty the rest of the day. The lost time will not be stopped out of your pay. Mr. Henley would like to speak to you as well. You may go straight up to the office. Do not tarry."

Without saying another word to the girls, he said to Gilbert, "I'll introduce you to the other investors." He took his arm and led him toward a frowning man with a withered-looking wife whose face was covered in white powder. "Perhaps you already know Godfrey Pallinger," he said when they'd drawn up to the couple.

"Indeed I do," Gilbert said, tipping his hat. Here was another man he wasn't keen on—a hard-horse sort of a fellow who looked as if he hadn't smiled in an eon or so. Pallinger had made his money in coal, and it was known to have blackened his heart. Gilbert had purchased prodigious quantities of that coal over the years and so was responsible for a portion of Pallinger's wealth, just as Pallinger was responsible for a portion of his own. The third investor, a solitary stranger named Jasper Pool, chewed a cigar and offered Gilbert a nod of the head by way of greeting.

Having been a steel magnate in his day, among other lucrative things, Gilbert had often philosophized upon the question of taking money from investors—whether one should look carefully at the source, or whether one should take what one was offered and look out of the window. He had regretted looking out the window early-on in his life, and had subsequently discovered that it wasn't necessary. Ill-gained money was not very much more common than honest money.

"Allow me to show you our collection of watermark stamps," Townover said to them, and without waiting for a reply they were off, looking over a vast display of wire filigree stamps, many of them of great age. Townover was obviously proud of the collection, and he pointed out the real gems, some of them centuries old. Each was mounted in a plain wooden frame. Gilbert himself had a tolerable collection of watermark stamps and paper, mainly Spanish. He had a particular eye for Faisán watermark paper, Faisán having specialized in bird watermarks, mostly waterfowl. He saw a good many examples of them here, and they elicited moderate feelings of greed. Samantha reappeared now, bowing demurely and silently presenting him with the colorful paper peacock.

"You are dismissed, Samantha," Townover said to her, and Sam put a smile on her face and bowed before walking off. The girl Daisy no longer sat at her workbench.

"She's a good lass, Samantha," Gilbert said. "I like her."

"To the contrary, she's lazy, and she's a ninny if she's allowed the opportunity to speak. Here now, gentlemen," he said to the lot of them, and he picked up three elegant wooden boxes from one of the shelves, the boxes worked with marquetry of silver and ebony. He handed a box to each of the men.

Gilbert discovered a ream of exquisitely textured, ivory-colored paper within his. He removed the top sheet and held it up to the light shining through the ceiling windows, and there, center top, was the image of a rampant hedgehog with a flailing red devil in its teeth—the Frobisher crest.

"I say!" Gilbert said happily. He smelled the paper, felt of it, nodded deeply, and thanked his host prodigiously.

Then they were away again, through a door in a bank of muslin-obscured windows, onto the mill floor and into a din of clattering sound and chemical stink. He heard Townover mutter a surprising curse, and saw that on one of the windows was a hastily scrawled skull and crossbones, clearly visible against the muslin beyond the glass. The bone-white paint was still shiny. A scattering of torn paper caps lay on the floor beneath the image. It was impossible to say whose caps they had been, however, because the Paper Dolls were steadily going about their business as if oblivious, all of them dressed in the requisite caps and aprons.

Chapter 7

You Won't Be Coming Back

D AISY SAT IN A wide rowing boat on the River Medway, making her lonely way home along the river's edge. A man and a boy were at the two sets of oars, making easy headway. She was bound for Aylesford, for the Chequers Inn, where she shared a small attic room with Clover Cantwell and Letty Benton, both Paper Dolls, although Letty had gone to London and hadn't returned two weeks past, so it was just she and Clover now. It was largely Clover's money that paid for the room, which was nicely private, although it cost more than living in the girls' dormitory in Snodland. Into her mind came the notion that in five minute's time, everything in her life had changed.

Daisy was three hours early leaving the mill, dismissed from her job because she was sick. It was for her own well-being, Mr. Henley had told her, but there were other sick Paper Dolls, the miasma having got into their lungs and skin, who were at their posts at this very instant. And there had been other sick girls who had been sent away—Letty for one—and like Daisy had not been allowed to say so much as a goodbye. Daisy had been hustled out the rear door by Mr. Jenks and driven in the chaise to the quay on the river.

She was exhausted now from the shortness of breath, which came in a wheeze most of the time, more painful as the day passed into evening, and she drew in the river air gingerly but gratefully. It was clean air and smelt of waterweeds and the tar and oakum that caulked the deck boards, heated by the afternoon sunshine. Beside her on the bench sat the only other passenger, an old woman carrying a basket on her lap. She was sound asleep, her chin on her chest. Daisy gazed at the arches of the old bridge and at the steeple of the Church of St. Peter and Paul and the back of the Chequers Inn along the river, where Mr. Swinton, the fat innkeeper, was busy at some task in the garden. Swallows darted over the water, which swirled slowly past, green and clear, the waterweeds and occasional silver fish passing beneath the boat.

She had been sent home with five twenty-pound banknotes in her pocket, more money than she had ever held in her hands before today. Mr. Henley had admonished her to say nothing to anyone about it for her own safety, and to deposit it in the Bank of England when she arrived in London tomorrow. Mr. Henley had also admonished her to be grateful, for it was a huge sum. But she was not grateful—not happy to leave Aylesford or to return to London and the squalor of her father's house. He would quickly have the money from her in any event, bank or no bank, and would drink it away. She had no idea where else to go, however.

The boat touched the stone dock beneath the bridge, and the boat's boy leapt out and tied the line fore and aft. The tide was in, the river flowing across all but the top two stairs. The boy, no more than ten years old, steadied her arm gallantly as she stepped out, and she favored him with a smile for his kindness. She wouldn't miss the mill, but she would miss Aylesford, which was a friendly place, unlike London. She was filled with a longing to remain. But tomorrow morning, when the Paper Dolls were awaiting the ferry on the wharf in Snodland, she would be bound for the unhappy place of her childhood.

She made up her mind in an instant as she walked up to the High Street: she would board the London train as she had been ordered, and then at a convenient station she would get off and board a return train back to Aylesford and make her way to Hereafter Farm. Henley Townover needn't know. He was a deeply hateful, heartless man, and it was none of his business to know.

She entered the inn, crossed the nearly empty tap-room, and ascended the stairs to her third-floor room. She lay down on her bed and fell asleep, awakening at dusk. Clover had failed to return from the mill—had gone to her aunt's house in Maidstone, perhaps. At eight o'clock Daisy went downstairs and ate supper, her raw throat so painful that she could scarcely swallow. She drank a half pint of porter to soothe it. Despite the nap she was utterly exhausted, and she could hear her own breathing, like a death rattle, it seemed to her, although she put the thought out of her mind.

She asked Mrs. Swinton, the landlady, to write a note to Mother Laswell at Hereafter Farm for her: that she had been dismissed from the mill and paid off, and was going into London on the morning train but would return at the first opportunity, perhaps in time for the soirée. She wondered if Mother Laswell would have any use for her on Hereafter, perhaps in the scullery now that her sister May had married and gone to live in Poole. She gave Mrs. Swinton a shilling piece when the message was written out, asking her whether the boy Henry might deliver it tomorrow and keep the shilling for his trouble.

"Happily," Mrs. Swinton said, taking the coin from her. "You're looking poorly, Daisy," she said. "You should toddle off to bed."

"I'm doing just that, Mrs. Swinton," she said, and she wearily climbed the narrow stairways, the gas-lamps hissing in their niches on the landings. She entered her room and closed the door behind her. A man stood there, staring at her—Mr. Davis from the mill, smiling in the low light. She turned as she trod backward toward the bed, which clipped her at the knees so that she sat down on it.

"Gather your things," Mr. Davis said.

"Mr. Henley told me that I was to board the *morning* train," Daisy told him breathlessly. She had never liked Davis, and he smelled of liquor now. But she had been told that it was Davis who would fetch her to the station in the morning, as if she couldn't find the way herself.

"Mr. Henley told you what he wanted you to know, Daisy. It's a chaise you'll be traveling in, not the train. Mr. Henley is concerned that you arrive at your destination safely."

"What destination? Am I to be left on the London streets in the darkness?"

"You'll be taken to a boarding house near St. Paul's. The landlady, Mrs. Thomas, is expecting you, no matter how late. You can stay with her as long as you like, given that you're a wealthy girl now. Mr. Townover has done his duty by you—ten times over, to my mind. Now pack your trunk. You won't be coming back."

Daisy moved the cloth and the water pitcher and bowl from the top of her small, flat-topped trunk, which had doubled as a low table. She gathered her few belongings, putting her paint box into a compartment on the bottom, and then packing her clothing and the few articles of her toilette. She put in her coat and her second pair of shoes and her old umbrella. After she clasped the trunk lid shut, Davis picked it up, set it on his shoulder, and waved her out of the room. She put her knit shawl on as she followed him down.

There were half a dozen men drinking beer in the taproom, and she could hear Mrs. Swinton clattering in the kitchen. Davis strode toward the door, the trunk angled across his shoulder, and it occurred to Daisy that he was hiding behind it, although at once she realized that it must be a foolish thought. Still and all, if Mrs. Swinton had known that a man had gone up to the attic, surely she would have remarked on it when she took the note. That might mean that Davis had sneaked in, and now he was leaving the same way, and she was leaving with him. For a moment she nearly bolted. But then the moment past, and the door had closed behind them.

They crossed the road, Davis taking her by the arm now, and up a dirt alley to where a chaise was standing, the horse tethered to a tree. Davis handed her up onto the seat, and in two minutes time he had strapped the trunk on behind, and the horse was carrying them across the old bridge. She told herself that the journey into London would delay her return only slightly. She looked behind her now, the lights of the village winking out as they rounded a bend in the road and entered the woods.

"You're wondering where we're bound, no doubt," Davis said to her. "It's Mr. Jenks that's taking you to London. He lives in Eccles with Mrs. Jenks."

"Ah," Daisy said. She had no idea that there *was* a Mrs. Jenks. She pulled her shawl more securely around her and wished that she hadn't put her coat into the trunk. She dared not ask Mr. Davis to stop for it, however, for he looked particularly brooding and unhappy, and he removed a flask from his coat and drank from it. He drove at what seemed to Daisy to be a dangerous pace along the road, which was dark as the grave now that they were in the deep shadow of the woods.

After ten minutes' travel he reined in the horses suddenly, although they were still a good distance from Eccles, and there were no houses roundabout, just trees and empty country. Away on the right stood a broad meadow up in flowers, and in the middle, black in the moonlight, were three standing stones, very ancient. A man stepped out from behind the stones, leading a horse, and her fears rushed back in upon her. It was the man Jenks. She saw him clearly enough to be sure—a short, brutish man who never had a kind word for the girls.

"I'll ask you for the packet of banknotes that Mr. Henley gave you," Davis said.

She looked at him, unable to speak, and a rush of bile rose in her throat. "Why?" she asked, knowing it was a foolish question, and in the next second she turned and threw herself off the edge of the seat. She felt Davis's hand paw at her back, and her shawl come away, but she was already running, gasping painfully. She saw Jenks pull himself into the saddle as she ran toward the tree line, holding her hand against her side where the banknotes were pinned to the waist of her dress. Jenks would cut her off. She saw that clearly, and she looked back and saw that Davis was still seated on the chaise, merely watching now, the outcome assured.

She ran on, hearing the horse's hooves, and she knew she was lost. Her shoe caught in a rabbit burrow and she was flung down, catching herself with her hands. She tried to scramble to her feet again, but Jenks's hands latched onto her clothing and she was yanked upright. She turned, swinging wildly at Jenks with her fist. She clipped him on the cheek, but he merely grinned at her. Her last sight on earth was of the moon in the sky above his shoulder and his closed fist rushing at her face.

Chapter 8

The Metaphoric Island

T HE SUMMER SOLSTICE WASN'T until tomorrow, but when it came to celebrations, neither Langdon St. Ives nor his wife Alice was a stickler for dates. The solstice was one of St. Ives's particular favorites, carrying with it the promise of long evenings spent in the garden, the children playing outdoors until after the badgers had come out of the sett and were busy in the evening dusk. He relished the reappearance of birds and animals that had been away for the winter. Just yesterday he had seen a honey buzzard, and last week a spotted crake. The world was particularly active in the early summer, when there was copious evidence that nature was going sensibly about her business, the earth abiding. Queen Victoria's Golden Jubilee had opened in London, but he wasn't tempted by it—had no desire to see it. The fish and birds and creatures of the woodland were oblivious to royalty and fanfare and so was he, the lot of them engaged in a never-ending jubilee of their own.

That thought brought to mind the several ringed plovers, summer bird visitors to England, which he and Hasbro had found dead on a shingly bank of the River Medway near Wouldham. Alice, a particularly avid fisherman, had caught two pike in the weir below the old bridge in Aylesford last week, both of the fish disfigured by tubercles and furry, discolored flesh. The effluent from the paper mill was heavier downstream, especially along the edge of the Wouldham marsh, but it was carried upstream to Aylesford as well, the Medway being a tidal river. He was thankful that the pond on their own property was fed by a spring, flowing since time immemorial, which provided water to irrigate the hops fields and the gardens. They were living on a variety of island, it seemed to him. And yet, St. Ives thought with a certain amount of nostalgic sorrow, islands were fragile things.

Their island, in fact, was changing its character. Hasbro and Mrs. Langley were to be wed in two week's time. For years Mrs. Langley had been the St. Ives's cook, housekeeper, and more recently nanny to the children. And now she was to become Mrs. Hasbro Dodgson.

Hasbro himself, once St. Ives's factotum—literally a man who might do anything and everything—had simply become his friend and companion. The years had done away with the idea of his being a servant of any variety. Given that he had independent means, St. Ives was happy that Hasbro and Mrs. Langley had elected to remain nearby. St. Ives could see the ragstone façade of their new home through the trees beyond the pond.

Mother Laswell's husband Bill Kraken, followed by Gilbert Frobisher's driver Boggs, emerged from the barn carrying a long, wooden table to add to the one already set up on the green along with a dozen or so chairs. Bowls of strawberries and shelled walnuts sat atop the first table, where Mother Laswell, dressed in a voluminous saffron-colored garment, sat opposite Gilbert Frobisher, a bottle of beer in front of each of them.

Hereafter Farm, Mother Laswell's domain, was a spiritualist commune along Bohemian lines with a distinct intolerance for any variety of cruelty, mean-spiritedness, or disregard for the natural world. Frobisher listened with an apparent show of interest to Mother's catalogue of complaints against the Majestic Paper Mill. Her women's society, Friends of the River Medway, had undertaken to go to war against the recalcitrant mill. It had been she who had asked St. Ives and Hasbro to collect water samples and dead animals along the river's shores, and St.

Ives had done so with a will. She was a good woman—an example to them all—but she had a way of involving those roundabout her, particularly St. Ives, in her troubles and intrigues. It was a flattering thing, really—she evidently had a high regard for him and Alice—but she sometimes seemed to be born to trouble as surely as sparks fly upward, to quote the book of Job.

St. Ives heard the cheerful sound of wooden batons knocking against pins from the direction of the skittles green, where Alice had taken up a challenge from Hasbro and Mrs. Langley. Clara Wright, one of Mother Laswell's charges and Finn Conrad's particular friend, was Alice's partner. Clara was blind, although she seemed to have—indeed, apparently *did* have—paranormal powers that lent her a sense of sight. She could throw a skittles baton with uncommon accuracy, taking aim with her outstretched elbow (through which she "saw") and then flicking the baton with a sideways motion that often enough knocked the pin out of the circle. Such things didn't stand to reason, but as Alice had pointed out, a baton knocking down a skittles pin was inarguable.

It came to St. Ives that he was sitting apart from his guests like an indifferent host, and so he found a bottle of beer for himself and joined Mother Laswell and Gilbert at the table. Gilbert pushed the walnut bowl toward him and said to Mother Laswell, "But do you see, ma'am, if

I was an investor I might induce them to make useful changes to the mill."

"Not at the expense of their almighty profits, you wouldn't, Mr. Frobisher," Mother Laswell told him evenly. "They've talked it back and forth until its been ironed flat, and there's been pieces written in the newspaper—sludge removal and charcoal filtration and that sort of thing. But it's mere rubbish. There's dead fish and dead birds to show for it, and sick girls, too. You told me of it yourself—poor Daisy Dumpel spewing blood. That mealy-mouthed Charles Townover is a withered stick of a man. He won't cram himself through the eye of God's needle, camel or no camel, and his hellfire son is worse. Men like that will drag you down to their level, Mr. Frobisher; you can't raise them up to yours. I'm heartily sick of bad men. I believe you to be one of the good ones, however. The Professor has told me that you built an entire wing of the Natural History Museum."

"Yes, ma'am, that is to say I *funded* the building of it—the *Bird Wing*, I like to call it, ha ha. I'll admit that I'm keen on preservation. I'm troubled by what you're telling me." He took several walnuts from the bowl and tossed them into his mouth.

"Then you'll attend tomorrow night's meeting of the Friends?" Mother Laswell asked. "There are interesting people coming down from London, and I've got an amusement planned. You'll hear Dr. Pullman's results and perhaps see the paper mill in a different light, despite the very fine box of paper you showed me. I have no argument with their paper, I can assure you. The Professor will attend our soirée. Isn't that so, Professor?"

"I will indeed," St. Ives said. "Alice is a member of the Friends, and so is Mrs. Langley."

"Then I'll be there," Gilbert said, although from St. Ives's perspective he appeared to be apprehensive. Mother Laswell's mention of "interesting people coming out from London" no doubt meant her friends from the Fabian Society and the Fellowship of the New Dawn, some of whom were vocal socialists and were recently taken up for sedition, although the charges had been dropped. Certainly it promised to be an entertaining evening by some definition of the word.

The conversation shifted to more neutral territory now, involving recent improvements that Alice and St. Ives had made to the grounds: indoor plumbing in the hoppers' huts, with a leach-field of rock and sand on low ground behind, which was now covered in blue-green clover...

St. Ives was interrupted by the laughter of his approaching children, Eddie and Cleo, who had taken an instant liking to the girl Larkin. Larkin was fond of the spoils that a life with the wealthy Gilbert Frobisher offered, but she hadn't lost her piratical flair, and had immediately made Cleo and Eddie a part of her crew. The children had ridden off toward Hereafter Farm aboard Dr. Johnson, the resident elephant, and they emerged now from the trees, riding easily on the elephant's ornate saddle. Finn Conrad, a young man who had fallen in with the St. Ives family several years ago and who lived in a cottage on the property, led the elephant by a halter, walking alongside Mrs. Tully, the wife of Hereafter's gardener. She saw Mother Laswell and hurried forward now. *Bad news*, St. Ives thought, seeing her face.

"The boy from the Chequers was out to the farm just now, ma'am," Mrs. Tully said when she drew up to the table. "He brought out a message and the daily news from Snodland and said it was important. I gave it a quick look and came a-running." She handed across a folded bit of foolscap and a copy of the Snodland *Gazette*.

Mother Laswell opened the note, read it to herself, and said, "Well, then! Daisy's quit the mill. She'll live at Hereafter. She's gone into London first, however." She looked up, shook her head, and said, "I wish the girl had come straight to me. Bill could have gone into London with her."

"Now the *Gazette*, ma'am," Mrs. Tully said uneasily.

Mother Laswell read over the front page silently, slumped back into her chair looking half destroyed and said, "We'll wait for the others, I believe, so that we don't have to consider this twice. Never mind the children, however. There's things children oughtn't to hear."

St. Ives saw that the skittles players were coming along in a group, and that Boggs and Bill Kraken were just now descending the kitchen stairs with immense meat pies on a platter and a vast tray of other dishes, steam rising from the lot of it. He wondered what piece of news was so vital that it had to be discussed at a celebration, but there was no polite way to put Mother Laswell off.

Alice came around behind him, squeezed his shoulder, and sat down. "It was a draw," she said breathlessly, "until Clara knocked out three pins one after another. We… What's amiss?" she asked Mother Laswell.

"It's Daisy Dumpel, Alice. Perhaps you remember her from the meeting two weeks ago?"

"Of course." Alice's smile had disappeared.

"Daisy is…*was* a Paper Doll from the Majestic Mill," she said to them. She studied the newspaper once again and then, pausing in between statements to read, she said, "Daisy was taken from her room in the Chequers Inn last night, accompanied by an unidentified man. She had told Mrs. Swinton of the Chequers that she possessed a ticket for this morning's train to London—which she told me the same in her note. She was murdered, however, and her body was found on the riverbank behind the tannery in Snodland. They've arrested her murderer, a union man who had been staying thereabouts by the name of Bill Henry. He'd been seen bothering Daisy two days back, as was reported to the Constable. Two mill hands found the man by chance in the Malden Arms. He was drunk and bragging on what he'd done, not knowing who he was talking to. Daisy had been let go from the mill and paid one hundred pounds as severance. This Bill Henry took it from her. It was in his pocket, in an envelope with Henley Townover's seal on it, which the constable found when he arrived. The man denied it, of course. That's the long and the short of it. He's confined in the Snodland jail."

The party sat quietly, giving Mother Laswell time to come to grips with the news. After a time, she said, "I wish the girl had come to me, poor child." She shook her head sadly. "The God-damned mill. Is there no end to it? My appetite has failed me, I'm afraid. Would it go too much against custom if I begged off, Professor?"

"No, indeed, ma'am," St. Ives said.

Alice helped Mother Laswell to her feet, and the company watched in silence as Bill and she set off arm-in-arm in the direction of Hereafter Farm, walking slowly, Mrs. Tully following along behind.

The silence was short-lived, however, for the children, having put Dr. Johnson away in the barn, came racing toward them across the green now, shouting with laughter and restoring equilibrium. They piled in around the table, holding out their hands to show that they'd washed away the elephant. Alice shushed them so that St. Ives could say a blessing over the food. The platters and bottles of wine started around the table, and St. Ives saw that Finn Conrad and Clara Wright were surreptitiously holding hands, both of them smiling. The *Gazette* still lay on the table, Daisy Dumpel's note sticking out of the pages like a bookmark. St. Ives picked it up and tucked it into his vest.

"God between us and all harm," he muttered, and right then he saw that there was a red deer in among the distant rose bushes, audaciously eating the yellow blooms in broad daylight. His first thought was to chase it off, but the thought filled him with self-doubt, and instead he wished the deer a good supper and a lucky passage and asked Alice to pass him the salt-cellar.

Chapter 9

The Burning

HEREAFTER FARMS, WITH ITS big stone house, its barn and commodious glass house and cottages, was alive with the glow of gaslamps and lanterns on the night of the soirée. It was a balmy night, and there was the phantom music of a violin on the air—Mr. Tully the musical gardener, no doubt, somewhere unseen. People stood about outdoors in groups, many of them holding glasses or bottles, and St. Ives could see that there were more revelers indoors as well, fifty or sixty people in all. He and Gilbert Frobisher stood before the door of the barn. St. Ives felt like an intruder, and Gilbert, perhaps, felt the same way, for he was uncharacteristically silent.

A photographer in a tall top-hat had set up his camera within a canvas enclosure. As St. Ives and Gilbert watched, a lavishly dressed woman with a long cigarette holder in one hand and a glass of champagne in the other sat down on the photographer's stool. The photographer said something to her, and she struck a pose. There was a flash of illumination from a hooded tin plate. She vacated the stool, and her place was taken by a man in evening clothes and wearing a monocle. Yet another man, this one with a pencil and note-book and with the look of a reporter about him, hurried after the woman with the cigarette holder, apparently trying to attract her attention.

"That rather lavish creature is Edith Nesbitt," Mother Laswell said to St. Ives and Gilbert, having come out of the barn door behind them, leading a grey mule by a rope. The mule was caparisoned in a colorful sort of shirt, and he wore a straw boater fastened beneath his neck with a ribbon.

"Should we have heard of Miss Nesbitt?" Gilbert asked. "I'm afraid that I'm abysmally uninformed when it comes to society, although I admire the ivory tube through which she smokes. The coal of the cigarette goes on before her like a lamp."

"She's married to Hubert Bland, the socialist and opium eater," Mother Laswell told them. "Married after a fashion, I should say. She's had children by the man in any event, as have several other women. She's an aspiring poet who writes tracts under the name Fabian

Bland. Quite an interesting specimen and a friend of Mr. Bernard Shaw, some say a very good friend indeed."

"It all sounds very Bohemian," Gilbert said. "Who is this fellow at the other end of the tether, then? I envy his hat."

"This is Ned Ludd, Mr. Frobisher."

"Himself?" Frobisher asked. "The wild-eyed destroyer of textile mills?"

"The very man, reincarnated as a mule. Our own Clara has taught him the alphabet."

"Good to make your acquaintance, Ned," Frobisher said to the mule, stroking the animal's neck. There was a gunpowder flash from the direction of the camera, and the mule rolled his eyes and shied sideways.

"Ned don't like the flash," Mother Laswell said. "Animals who live in straw have a hatred of fire."

"Eminently sensible," St. Ives said. He saw that Alice, Mrs. Langley, and Clara Wright were approaching the environs of the camera. "Is the photographer a local man, then?" he asked.

"I admit that I don't know," Mother Laswell said. "I surely did not summon him. He must have come down from London with the others. Some of these celebrities are quite vain, you know. But I must hurry away, gentlemen. The Friends of the River Medway had best be photographed together. We could do with some celebrity

of our own. No hiding beneath a bushel basket for us."
Leading Ned Ludd, she hurried off to join Alice and Mrs.
Langley for a photographing.

"Do they hang capitalists in this part of the world?"
Frobisher asked.

"Not commonly," St. Ives said. "I myself have never
been to a meeting of Mother Laswell's Society, however,
so I can't swear that a hanging is unusual. You and I will
be outsiders together. They'll have to hang the both of us."

"I'm relieved to hear you say that, brother. She seems
to believe that I'm a right thinker, but this is monu-
mentally strange to me. Tubby is always insisting that I
should listen rather than speak, but of course I generally
pay him no mind. Tonight, however, I'll heed his advice.
Listening rarely insults anyone's sensibilities."

"I'll follow your example," St. Ives said. He saw Dr.
Pullman now, just then drawing up in his wagon. "I'll
introduce you to Lamont Pullman," he said to Gilbert.
"He's an eminent naturalist as well as the local coroner, and has been looking into the depredations of the
Majestic Paper Mill." They approached Dr. Pullman,
a small man who wore a discreditable laboratory coat
stained with unidentifiable substances. After Pullman
and Frobisher had shaken hands, the three men exam-
ined the many jars on Pullman's wagon, each containing a
poisoned bird, fish, or amphibian floating in preservative

spirits. Dr. Pullman pointed out cankers and areas of rotted or discolored flesh, all of the damage consistent with the poisons in the water samples taken from Eccles Brook, downstream from the mill. St. Ives could see that Frobisher was deflated by what he saw. The evidence was inarguable. They carried the lot of them indoors and uncrated them.

Very soon Mother Laswell herded the assembled guests into the house, drawing their collective attention to the jars. St. Ives and Frobisher shifted into a far doorway to listen to Dr. Pullman's address to the gathering. St. Ives heard little that he did not already know, except for a general confirmation. He heard mutters of disapproval roundabout him, however, including from Gilbert himself.

Mother Laswell followed Pullman's account with a general call for action against the enormities of the mill and passed out a pamphlet promoting the work of the Friends of the River Medway. She thanked Dr. Pullman and led the crowd outdoors again, through the open French windows toward the back of the house, where a broad meadow stretched away in the direction of the woods. St. Ives saw at once that the meadow was to be the site of the "amusement."

"I'm in a pickle," Gilbert said to him when they'd found a convenient place from which to watch. "I've told Charles Townover that I'll be up to see him tomorrow about the investment. But I find that I cannot. This is not as simple as it had seemed, and if there's trouble at the mill it'll tar me with that same brush, or some variety of filthy brush. I believe that I'll tell him I'm ill in order to gain some time. I'll send a message."

"You're wise to do so. Here's something, though. I've been thinking that I might go up to the mill tomorrow myself to have a look at the man. Would it be sensible for me to introduce myself as your friend? I could convey your message, extend your regrets, and it might open a door that might otherwise be closed to me."

"You have no scruples against telling a small untruth on my behalf?"

"None whatsoever," St. Ives said. "Finn Conrad would happily show you the resident birds tomorrow. There's a particularly cheerful owl in one of the oaks."

"Capital. Ah!" he said, gesturing with his forehead. "There's Mother Laswell getting set to amuse us."

The meadow grasses had been scythed flat, so that the area looked something like a cricket pitch. Makeshift wooden tables sat around the perimeter, each with a lantern in the center, and people had made their way to the tables now and crowded around them, laughing and talking. On the green itself sat pasteboard buildings, six of them, the walls waist-high, the buildings connected by pasteboard walkways and fences, all of it realistically painted, right down to the roof slates. There were windows and doors cut into the buildings, along with chimneys and stairways. There was a carriage house and barn— all of it accurate, at least as St. Ives remembered it from his adventures on the premises of the mill several nights back. A banner stretched between two wooden poles over the top of the construction read, "Majestic Paper Mill." Paper bunting swooped away from the banner to the roofs of the various buildings.

"This is Mother Laswell's work," St. Ives said to Frobisher. "She has artistic talents."

"She's done a thoroughgoing job of it," Gilbert said. "She's even got the skylights in the roof." I cannot imagine why she's gone to the trouble, given that she loathes the place."

Mother Laswell herself strode into the center of the green along with Bill Kraken. Kraken, who most often had a barmy look about him, with unkempt hair and a singularly crooked gait that made him appear to be staggering along in a gale-force wind, was comparatively well groomed. He was dressed in a waistcoat and embroidered vest, and had a battered bowler hat pulled down low over his forehead. He carried something in his hand—a rush torch, from the look of it.

Mother Laswell had donned a flowing purple robe with a wash of stars across the bodice. She stood beneath the starry sky with her hand upraised, looking like a figure in an illustration. She waved the crowd silent and began to speak in a powerful voice.

"Moments ago you saw with your own eyes a collection of poisoned animals—a mere trifle compared to the thousands that have passed away down the River Medway to the sea. Now you behold before you a replica of the Majestic Paper Mill, which expels its filthy poisons into the River, unhindered by law or common decency." She paused to let this resonate, and then said, "This model was assembled to nearly exact proportions according to figures given to me by a lovely girl named Daisy Dumpel, who worked at the mill and was made sick by it. Yesterday Daisy was found *murdered*. Who murdered her? I can tell you that the man *accused* of the crime was found hanged in his cell this very morning—out of remorse, the newspapers tell us. Perhaps it's the truth. Or perhaps it is part of a greater lie. Perhaps an innocent man and an innocent girl have been murdered by *men who would sell their souls to gain the world!*"

St. Ives hadn't heard about the hanging, and it struck him as odd—too convenient by half—a girl murdered and her alleged murderer very quickly dead into the bargain, the case fortuitously solved, or at least disposed of. Mother Laswell's *perhaps it's the truth* was evidently laced with irony, and well it might be. He wondered whether Mother herself was treading on thin ice, however, shouting out her suspicions to the world. She was in the right, of course, generally speaking. He would admit that readily. But her Society was made up of more persons than herself, and she presumed to speak for them all, bolstered by what she considered the unassailable rightness of her position.

She held up her hands now, quieting the crowd, who were engaged in a cacophony of discussions, some of them drunken discussions, to be sure. She nodded to Kraken, who struck a Lucifer match on his shoe sole and set ignited the wax-filled rushes. *"Burn it!"* Mother Laswell commanded, and Kraken set fire to the banner, which burst into bright flame. The two of them strode off to the nearest table as the flames ignited the bunting, the fire diminishing somewhat as it crept down to the buildings themselves, but then spreading quickly across the pasteboard slates of the rooftops. St. Ives wondered what the banner and bunting had been soaked in to make it burn so—paraffin, perhaps.

The walls of the mill flared up and collapsed inward, the flames leaping. One by one the other buildings followed suit, until all were in varying stages of collapse. People began to cheer and applaud, many of them holding their glasses up in a general toast. St. Ives saw that the photographer was hastily stowing his gear into his wagon with the help of a boy who appeared to be ten or twelve years old, and very soon the two of them hauled the wagon across the green, apparently in a hurry to get out ahead of the rest of the crowd. After a time the fires flickered out, leaving the night dark despite the lantern light. The beauty of the starry sky and of the dark wood behind the meadow contrasted sharply with the ugly smell of the burning.

Chapter 10

The Right Side of Things

T HE HOUSE WAS QUIET, the children down for the night, or pretending to be, on cots in the sleeping gallery. They had wanted to sleep in the barn with the elephant and the owls and bats—Larkin had been going to teach them how to kill rats with a throwing stick—but Alice and Gilbert had agreed that the summer solstice was a rat holiday in Kent and that the rats should be given a reprieve.

"It's odd that the world is a private place within the confines of the bed curtains," Alice said. "It's very like being in a tent in the forest, isn't it? Or cast away upon an island. One supposes that one can say or do almost anything without anyone overhearing or taking notice."

"Funny you should say such a thing," St. Ives said. "I was contemplating on islands just yesterday—how we lived upon one in a sense—an enchanted island, especially in this season of the year." They lay looking up at the candle-lit canopy—a tapestry figured with the night sky seen through leaves and boughs, the corners of the sky fixed to the tall bedposts. The warm night breeze shifted the window curtains, which, along with the bed curtains on that side, were drawn aside to give them a view.

Both of them had been reading, but St. Ives put down his book now, and said, "I have mild misgivings about this affair of Mother Laswell's. Her anger is well founded, of course, but she made use of very heavy artillery, so to speak. And as for the London crowd, they kept the reporter intrigued, but I cannot see how they were an asset to her cause. She asked for no contributions, after all. I can tell you that Gilbert came away looking unnerved."

"An asset to *our* cause, in fact," Alice said. "Yours and mine. All of ours." She gestured with a copy of *Murphy's Fishing Catalogue*, which she was in the habit of perusing with something like greed. "Mother believes that the cause must be made public. Surely your doubts are not meant to suggest that I abandon her? Men talk a great deal about honor, but honor is a commodity that women value as well, you know."

"Yes, of course, but perhaps you can convince her that it's in her best interests to…"

"Mother is convinced that the newspaper account of poor Daisy's murder is false, and so her own best interests are of no particular importance to her, which should come as a surprise to neither of us."

"Still, the burning of the mill was moderately shocking, given that it was the Majestic Paper Mill down to its particulars. The photographer took photos of it, of course, and the wandering reporter scribbled notes. When the business is made public, as you say, it will look very much like a threat."

"Mother will insist that the burning was merely symbolic, which of course it was."

St. Ives looked out through the window curtains at the night sky. A white bird flew into view and then out again, a barn owl no doubt. "I've found that a person can be in the right but be made to look wrong. The newspapers have made a study of it."

"And yet that has never stopped you from putting yourself on the right side of things when it was safer to walk away."

He had no answer to this, or to any of it, and sat looking at the dancing candle flame now. After a few moments Alice went back to her catalogue.

"Do you know what gives me pause?" he asked, interrupting her reading once again.

"I do not," she said, "unless it's a newt. You regularly pause over newts."

"I'm quite serious. It was alleged that the murderer possessed one hundred pounds in an envelope that he had taken from the girl Daisy, and that the money was given to her by the Majestic Paper Mill for reasons that aren't at all clear. Robbery is the implied motive for the murder, or at least one of the motives. But surely no girl in Daisy's position would reveal to a man she's only recently met that she has one hundred pounds about her person."

"It's said that she left the Chequers in the man's company willingly enough, so she must have trusted him."

"And yet, according to Dorothea Swinton at the Chequers, Daisy wrote the message to Mother Laswell not fifteen minutes before she was seen leaving the inn with the murderer, and Charles Townover, the mill owner, confirmed that Daisy had been going to leave for London on the morning train. Why this confusion?"

Alice shrugged. "Perhaps this man prevailed upon her to change her mind about going into London. Girls have been tricked and abused by men since the dawn of time."

"But no one in the taproom saw the man's face, because he was carrying Daisy's trunk on his shoulder," St. Ives said. "She apparently had no idea of leaving her room at the Chequers that night. Surely she would have told Mrs. Swinton if she had instead of insisting that she was to leave in the morning. If it was this Henry fellow who convinced her to leave with him, he accomplished the feat in record time. Something's amiss. There are pieces to the puzzle that went into the river with the girl's body."

"I believe that entirely," Alice said to him. "I wonder why was she given such a grand sum at the mill?"

"Perhaps because they were intent upon buying her silence."

They were both quiet for a time, having worn out the conversation with unanswerable questions. They blew out their respective candles, and in the darkness watched the drifting, moonlit clouds and the winking stars.

"But if they bought Daisy's silence," Alice asked after a time, "why would they have had her throttled and thrown into the river?"

"There you have me," St. Ives said.

Chapter 11

The Investigation

THE RAILWAY PLATFORM LOOKED out onto the River Medway through the trees. The river was low, with broad mudflats. St. Ives found the railway porter easily enough, a man he had said good-day to many times over the past couple of years, and he discovered now that the man's name was Jeffries. Porters, he had long ago discovered, were founts of knowledge.

"I seen him right enough, sir," Jeffries told him, "a small man with a top-hat like a stove pipe, meant to raise his stature I don't doubt, and a small, worthless boy alongside, although all the same your man oughtn't to have kicked the boy. It was me who hauled his hat trunk out to the road. It weren't full of hats, but photographic equipage. Heavy, it was, not a proper hat trunk, but with a thick wooden bottom in it. A man in a wagon drove him and his goods away, and the boy with them. I can tell you the man's name, if you like, for I saw it on his trunk."

"I would like that very much, yes."

"Manfred Pink, it was. An odd name, I thought, although there were some Pinks living around Hastings when I was a boy."

"Did Pink come in on one of the London trains, then? There were a number of passengers from London stopping yesterday, if I'm not mistaken."

"You make no mistake," Jeffries told him. "They came down for the doings at Hereafter. But your man didn't come down with the rest of the toffs. He came up from Tunbridge Wells in the morning, as I know because he told me himself. It was a *Dockett's* hat trunk that he carried, very pricey. Mr. Dockett, the old man, was a friend of my Uncle Jennings, and many's the time I sat in Dockett's shop as a boy in Tunbridge Wells. Old man Dockett would give me leather scraps and brass fittings. The point is I told your man that a Dockett's was a first-rate trunk, just to be civil, and he said he knew it well enough already, living in Tunbridge Wells as he did, nigh Dockett's shop, and he hadn't asked for my approval. That was your small man with the top-hat—a man who can't speak civil and who kicks boys because they can't afford to kick him back."

A train came into the platform now with a whoosh of steam brakes and a loud screeching. The doors opened, and scattered passengers stepped off. St. Ives gave Jeffries a half crown and received a tip of the hat in response before Jeffries turned away to help a woman with a spray of feathers in her bonnet, taking up her bag and guiding her down the platform, warning her to take particular care.

St. Ives followed them, knowing exactly what he had come to find out, but wondering what it meant: a photographer from Tunbridge Wells, whom Mother Laswell hadn't summoned, had descended upon the soirée apparently of his own accord. It was apparent that the London revelers had relished having their photographs taken, but there was no sign that they knew the man or that they had any expectations of him.

———

St. Ives was shown into the entry hall at the Majestic Paper Mill by a girl wearing a paper hat and apron. She gave him a paper swan, curtsied indifferently, and went away. He stood with his hat and swan in his hand for a bare two minutes before Charles Townover came out to meet him, ushering him to a chair and taking another himself, a broad desk between them. The interior of the mill was as Gilbert had described it—clean and well lit. A great deal of money had been spent on amenities. Beyond a long bank of windows draped with muslin there were signs of activity—paper being made within the mill proper. If it weren't for the unpleasant reek of chemicals and the sound of the machinery, it would almost have been a welcoming place, at least on this side of the glass.

"I come on behalf of my friend Gilbert Frobisher," St. Ives said to Townover after the man had re-introduced himself, apparently having forgotten that he had met St. Ives in the past. "Regrettably, he's been taken ill, and he won't be able to meet with you and the other investors this afternoon."

"That's unfortunate, indeed," Charles Townover said, giving St. Ives an appraising look. "And you've come up the river from Aylesford to inform me of this? You must have remarkably little to do. It would have saved you a mort of trouble if Frobisher had sent a message. *You* might have sent the message, for that matter."

"I have business in Snodland, actually, so it was no trouble at all. Mr. Frobisher also asked that I relay his regret about the unfortunate incident of the murdered girl. She had made him a paper peacock, as I understand it."

"We all regret the incident, sir, but the man who perpetrated the crime has hanged himself, and so some virtue has come of it."

"He was associated with a union, then, the murderer? So I read in the *Gazette*."

Townover stared at him, and it came to St. Ives that he might have overreached himself. "I mean to say that it's a black mark against a union," he said, "to send such a man to do its business."

"A union's business is a black mark upon itself," Townover told him, "and it doesn't surprise me a bit that its emissaries are blackguards. You would do me a favor to convey to Mr. Frobisher that the Majestic Paper Mill does not require the encouragement of a union. We think of ourselves as a family. Simply put, Daisy Dumpel was a member of that family, and this union man—*disunion* being more to the point—murdered a girl who was in my charge. The girls know that they can come to me with their troubles, just as they would go to their own fathers. This is the essence of my meeting this afternoon with the investors, or a part of it."

St. Ives nodded agreeably, deciding to probe a little more deeply, even at the hazard of ending things: "Mr. Frobisher will be happy to hear it. He was pleasantly surprised at the largesse displayed by the mill to the Dumpel girl. One hundred pounds is quite a sum."

"Yes, it is," said Townover. "My point exactly. What sort of business brings you into Snodland, sir?"

"I grow hops. I like to keep in touch with local brewers. It adds an air of familiarity and good cheer to business dealings."

"That would be Crosland, then? Hillhurst Crosland? The Crown Brewery?"

"The very man," St. Ives lied. He actually sold his hops to the Anchor Brewery in Aylesford and had no dealings at all with the Crown Brewery.

"Then give him my best wishes. I've known him for some time. And convey those same wishes to Gilbert Frobisher. Tell him that I'm anxious to speak with him as soon as he's well."

Townover leaned back in his chair and folded his hands, the conversation apparently at an end. The door from the mill floor opened, and a tall, horse-faced man came out, saw them, and headed in their direction. St. Ives recognized him immediately, his tweed cap as well, from that night along the Eccles Brook, but he meant to deny anything the man might accuse him of.

"What is it, Davis?" Townover asked him, but Davis was staring at St. Ives with what was clearly a look of surprise on his face, although it faded quickly.

"Do we know each other?" St. Ives asked him.

"I thought we might, but I see I was mistaken. I'm sorry to interrupt."

"Our conversation was at an end, Davis," Townover said. And then to St. Ives, he said, "I have a business to attend to, sir. The door stands yonder. I regret that none of the girls are on hand to show you out, sir, so you'll have to find your own way."

———

WHEN THE DOOR was shut behind St. Ives, Charles Townover looked carefully at Davis as if taking his measure. "Did you in fact recognize that man?" he asked.

"No, sir. I did not. When I first saw him he looked something like a gent I knew in London, but when I came up to him I seen it wasn't so."

"You're quite sure of that? He had a look on his face when he saw you that I couldn't quite fathom. He hid it away immediately, however."

"I'm sure I don't know, sir. I've come to say that Mary Shanks has puked blood into the vat, and that Jenks is pumping it out. The girl is gone to the infirmary."

"I'll pay her a visit. I want you to do me a service, however. Have a look out the window upstairs to ascertain whether Mr. St. Ives turns upriver toward the Wouldham Bridge or downriver toward Aylesford. If he's bound for Snodland and means to cross the bridge, I want you to follow him on horseback. But tether the horse and take the ferry across to the wharf so that he doesn't see you crossing the bridge behind him. Do not molest the man in any way. Do not so much as speak to him. He's a friend of Gilbert Frobisher, who is potentially very valuable to us as an investor. I have no intention of causing Frobisher's friends any grief, no matter how meddlesome they are. St. Ives says that he is bound for the Crown Brewery. If that turns out to be true, then return to the mill. If it is not true, then I want to know where he goes."

"Yes, sir," Davis said, and turned away toward the stairs.

"Davis! One more thing! If, as I suspect, he is *not* bound for the brewery, then allow yourself to be seen, but do *not* speak to the man. I merely want him to know that I have my eye on him."

St. Ives was certain that Davis had recognized him. Hasbro had remained in Aylesford in order to make that less likely, but the gaff had been blown, and there was no help for it now. Davis had no doubt informed Townover as soon as St. Ives was out of the building. It came to him that he would be clearly visible from the upper windows of the mill, and so decided that he would turn north toward the bridge at Wouldham if only to allay some of the old man's suspicions. He would avoid being caught in an obvious lie, and he would look into the pub at the Malden Arms on his way back upriver, where the alleged murderer had been run to ground. The murder and hanging were not his affair, but his curiosity had been piqued.

He had the confirmed feeling that Townover had told him the truth as he knew it, and might have said more if St. Ives hadn't started in on him like the Grand Inquisitor. It would have been wise to move more slowly. Townover believed in himself and in the mill, and he believed that the murder of Daisy Dumpel was yesterday's news, although despite the talk of the mill "family," he seemed to have no apparent pity for the murdered girl. Perhaps he was like old Scrooge in the story, the pity having gone out of him over the years, replaced by an armor of self-righteousness.

He crossed the bridge a short time later, the tide rising now, carrying an unsettling number of dead birds and fish, which could conveniently be seen from above. He made his way upriver again into Snodland proper, the ferry dock on his left hand and the tannery beyond, where Daisy's body had been found on the mud bank. He turned up Ferry Road, past the back of the jail, and then up the tree-lined High Street, where he saw the sign for the Malden Arms, a white-painted, three-story inn with green shutters. There was the smell of frying bacon from the open taproom door, and, unmistakably, of coffee beans roasting in a pan. He reined up, persuaded by his stomach, and handed over the horse and buggy to the stable boy.

The paneled room was pleasantly dim, with seafaring paintings on the walls and an expertly built miniature of a ship of the line on the fireplace mantel. Three tables were occupied, two of them by men reading newspapers and third by a man and a woman who were eagerly devouring plates of eggs and rashers and beans. The publican, a heavy-set man with long mustaches and heavy spectacles, stood polishing glasses behind the bar. He nodded in a friendly manner when St. Ives asked for breakfast and coffee. After speaking through the window to the cook, he asked St. Ives whether he was staying upstairs.

St. Ives admitted that he was not, but had stopped in because it was a likely looking inn and because of the smell of the roasting coffee beans. He looked around in general appreciation, like a man in no particular hurry. "I'll admit," he said, "that I read of the Malden Arms in the *Gazette*. Two men from the mill caught the murderer here, as I understand it."

"Aye, Davis and Jenks, both of them regular customers," the publican said, dumping roasted beans into a mortar and grinding them. "This Bill Henry, he'd been in once or twice. He didn't have the look of a murderer to me, but people are like books, in that regard, if you take my meaning. Do you like a *strong* cup of coffee?"

"I do," St. Ives said, "and I take your point about people and books. Take Admiral Nelson as an illustration. He was a small little man with one arm, but he beat the stuffing out of the French and the Spanish at Trafalgar."

"So he did, too. He didn't have the look of a hero about him. That said, a Frenchman shot him dead with a musket ball, which was dumb luck, although what that says about books, I don't know. Mayhaps that's all we have as an ending once we've read through the chapters." He put a heap of grounds into a china pot, pouring hot water over them and letting them steep. He set the pot, a cup, and a finely meshed sieve-disk in front of St. Ives, and then leaned against the bar. "The *Gazette* was wrong about one thing, however. They caught this Bill Henry in the alley behind, not inside. He saw them come in and when they went for him, he bolted. They tackled him in the alley and thrashed him."

"That's justice," St. Ives said, "If he was a guilty man."

"When the hue-and-cry went up, Constable Bates came running. It was he who found the girl's money in Bill Henry's coat. Davis said that he'd seen Henry bothering the girl at the mill, and the two things were enough to lock him up, although maybe not to hang him. He did that to himself with his own gaiters, however, and that condemns him, I suppose. An innocent man don't hang himself."

"That's certain," St. Ives said, thinking about this. His breakfast arrived now, the food steaming on the plate, a rack of toast and a tiny bowl of jam. The publican poured coffee into his cup through the sieve, and it seemed to St. Ives that coming into Snodland was a useful business all the way around.

"Speak of the devil," the publican said in a surprised tone of voice, looking at the open door.

St. Ives looked in that same direction, his coffee cup halfway to his mouth, just in time to see Davis's head looking in at him. Davis tipped his tweed hat, winked, and disappeared from the doorway.

———

"Yes, sir." Davis said to Charles Townover, Davis having just returned from Snodland. "He went into the village and straight to the Crown. I waited out of sight until he came back out, and then followed him to the river. He turned upriver toward Aylesford, the way he'd come down, and I followed along after at a good distance until I was sure he was homeward bound. He did just as he said he would."

Townover considered this, looking steadily at Davis. "You're certain?" he said. "He made no other stops?"

"As certain as I'm standing here."

"And you do *not* know this fellow St. Ives? From London or from anywhere else?"

"No sir. I take my oath on it."

Townover nodded. "I don't like him, and I believe him to be false. Communicate this to Henley when he arrives and see whether he has anything useful to say, both about this St. Ives and about Mary Shanks. I fully believe that the girl spoiled the vat intentionally. She could as easily have vomited onto the floor. It's past time to rout out troublemakers."

Chapter 12

The Broadsheet

CLOVER WALKED ALONG THE lane toward Hereafter Farm. The day was warm and the road was dusty, and she was happy for the shade of the over-arching oaks and for the grassy verge. A rill of water hurried along beside, its bed brown with leaves from the oaks, but the water clear. No one had passed her since she had turned off the road, which wasn't surprising, since Hereafter Farm sat at the dead-end of its own lonely lane. She heard children whooping not too far ahead, and she slowed her pace and looked cautiously about, anxious not to be seen until she wanted to be seen.

Twenty yards farther on, the corner of a barn showed through the trees. Two children dashed past it and disappeared. The lane broadened out into a carriage drive of packed dirt and gravel, and beyond it stood a two-story house of grey stone with a broad front porch. She stepped behind the trunk of a tree and watched the house, considering what she should do. Henley had sent her to discover what she could, but there was precious little she'd discover if she weren't a sneaker. She was particularly good at sneaking.

There was enough sunlight on the porch for her to see that the door to the house stood open, and right now there was no one about. She could hear flies buzzing and the sound of laughter—the children again—but she couldn't see them. She stepped out and walked toward the house, looking about curiously, which would seem natural if she were observed, and without a pause she climbed the stairs and crossed to the open door as quietly as she could. She hesitated at the door, hearing a conversation within, several voices. They were having a regular powwow.

Clover stepped into the kitchen, the voices growing louder, and she moved to a door that led into a hallway. It occurred to her that she could load her bag with valuables and walk out if she chose, but it would be short sighted, to be sure. She walked quietly down the hallway, past two empty rooms, until she stood by what must be the parlor, trying to decide whether to knock against the door moulding to announce herself, or to bide her time and listen.

—⁓—

THE REMAINS OF their tea sat on a wheeled cart, nothing but two broken biscuits and a last quarter of sandwich, still unclaimed. St. Ives was fond of afternoon tea when he could afford the time it took to consume it in a civilized manner, which was rarely. Today he had eaten nothing since his breakfast at the Malden Arms. Mrs. Tully's deviled ham made capital sandwiches, and Bill Kraken had just opened a second bottle of sherry. The lot of them sat in the parlor at Hereafter Farm, laying out a plan of action, although Mother Laswell had particularly strong opinions, and the plan shifted this way and that way with her enthusiasms. She meant to make a speech to the girls at the mill, she said, in order to move them to action. They were apparently ripe for it. If the girls walked out, it would open Pandora's Box, and everything else would follow.

"And I fully intend to be ready when it does," she said. "I've composed an article for the *Gazette*, with evidence laid out so that any fool can see the sense in it. Poisons will kill the River Medway if the mill is allowed free rein, including the oyster beds in Long Reach and Sheerness in time. The river won't return to its glory, not in our lifetime, unless we act." She slapped the arm of her upholstered chair and nodded sharply. "It's a call to arms.

I mean to throw an iron plow into the workings of the mill, by God, if that be the only means at our disposal."

"Don't speak rash," Bill Kraken said to her. "You're asking to be taken up and thrown into Newgate Prison, and then you'll see precious little more in your lifetime and never mind oysters."

"Someone's got to speak rash, Bill, and to twist their noses if they won't heed. How else will we stop them?"

St. Ives had little to say to this, although Kraken was quite possibly correct. Townover would make concessions to conciliate the Friends of the River Medway, but he surely would not hesitate to resist any heavy-handed efforts to force his hand. Mother Laswell had the passion of the true believer, and assumed that others would rally round, but others rarely did. People disliked agitation, for the most part, especially those who were being agitated against.

St. Ives looked out the French windows now and saw Eddie, Cleo, and Larkin astride the long-suffering Ned Ludd, sneaking along the wall of the barn carrying bows and arrows that Kraken had made for them. The arrows were capped with chunks of india-rubber affixed with hide glue. Another clump of children had disappeared into the barn a few minutes back—three of Mother Laswell's orphan children—no doubt setting up an ambush. He envied their innocence. Long may it reign, he thought.

"Come, Professor," Mother Laswell said to St. Ives, "Alice tells us that you went into the mill itself to beard Charles Townover in his den. What did you discover?"

"Nothing useful. I'm afraid that I simply drew the attention of the man. I was ham-handed in my dealings with him. I apologize for that, Gilbert."

"Not at all," Frobisher said. "This morning I decided to give up any notion of investing in the mill, *if* that's the general consensus. I'll send news to Townover this very evening if you wish."

He looked around a little bit unhappily, or so it seemed to St. Ives, who said, "Perhaps if your illness persisted for a few more days, the *promise* of your investing might yet have some influence over the man. I came away with the feeling that he might see reason, that he doesn't mean entirely ill, but is merely reacting, if you take my meaning."

"I do not," Mother Laswell said. "I believe that he means very ill indeed."

"Begging your pardon, ma'am, but I'm of the same mind as the Professor," Gilbert said to her. "Charles Townover is doing harm, certainly, but perhaps he could be convinced to cease doing so. He has the self-righteousness of a man who believes himself to be correct. He's been singularly successful in his life, after all. Now he perceives himself to be under siege. I don't like him, but he hasn't come as far as he has without being able to see through a window."

"What would you have us do, then, Mr. Frobisher?" Mother asked. "I, too, can see through a window, although the window at hand is tolerably filthy, if you take my meaning."

"I take it very seriously, ma'am. But I'll tell you what I mean to do, now that you ask…"

Frobisher nodded and stroked his chin, then seemed surprised to see that his sherry glass stood half full. He picked it up, contemplated it, and then drank it off in a single swallow. "I came up to Kent with the idea of investing in fine paper," he said, standing up now, as if he was addressing an assembly. "I found that very article at the Majestic Paper Mill—very fine paper indeed, and many people employed…"

"Fine paper traded for disease and death," Mother Laswell said, interrupting him. "It's a Devil's bargain."

"Yes, ma'am. I don't deny it. But what if there was *no* disease and death? What if we turn the Devil out of doors? I propose to offer Townover a significant sum, but on the assurance that my investment would be spent to carry out the aims of the Friends of the Medway—to civilize the mill, so to speak. The man would be nothing out of pocket. Gilbert Frobisher would bear the cost, but the newspapers would cry up Charles Townover as a hero, and his fortunes would improve. The mill would be an example to the world. What do you think, Professor? Can the thing be done?"

"I believe so—with a sufficient outlay of money. A great deal can be done with simple sedimentation if the effluent can be contained over a proper field. We would have to consult with people who know more about these things."

"Then it must be done quickly, I believe," Mother Laswell said, "or else the Medway will be as dead as Lazarus and we've got nothing left to us but prayer."

"Then we'll consult with all our might, by gad," Frobisher said, reaching for the sherry bottle. "Townover will see reason. The mill will change its character, do you see, and so will the man, once he perceives the profit in it. He's a man of business, after all."

⸻

CLOVER LISTENED FROM the shadows of the hallway, stowing away the details of the conversation. She would like to have seen the people speaking, but there was no real need to take the chance of peering around the doorjamb. She heard something behind her now—the rustle of a skirt? She felt a presence and she turned, looking down the dim hallway. Ten feet away from her stood a young woman of about her own age. She was blind, her milk-white eyes peering forward. She stood very still, and it seemed to Clover that she might have been standing so for a time.

Clover looked away from her and stepped boldly forward into the parlor. The fat man who had been speaking fell silent, and she gave him the prettiest smile she could manage. "I don't mean to interfere," she said. "The front door stood open, and one of the children told me to step in. I'm a friend of Daisy Dumpel, a Paper Doll at the mill, just as she was. We had a room at the Chequers together. I've come from there to see Mother Laswell."

"*I* am Mother Laswell," the heavy-set woman dressed in robes said—something Clover already knew, since the broadsheet that Clover carried had several likenesses of the woman. A disheveled looking man with a windstorm of hair and who reminded her of an underfed mongrel dog sat next to her. He gave Clover a suspicious look. He would be trouble, she thought. He was probably born for it. The dark haired woman was Alice St. Ives: her likeness was on the broadsheet also.

Mother Laswell looked past her now, and Clover knew without turning around that the blind girl had followed her. It mattered little, however. Clover meant to have her say and leave, and she had no idea of returning to this place unless Henley compelled her to.

"What is your name, child?" Mother Laswell asked, regarding her more keenly now.

"Clover Cantwell, ma'am. People call me Clo sometimes."

"And why have you come, Clo? You're welcome here, of course, but you must have had a long walk."

"Yes, ma'am. Daisy told me of you and your society about the river, and so when the man left these papers off in the taproom at the Chequers, I told Mrs. Swinton that you'd want to see them because of what they say. The boy at the Chequers was away with the gig, however, and wasn't expected back until late, so I walked. It isn't far. I walk to Maidstone to see my Aunt Gower most Sundays."

"And what can you tell us about Daisy?" Mother Laswell asked. "The newspapers revealed her name, but said little else."

"Well, I guess I'll say that Daisy was mending, but Mr. Townover feared for her health, and so he gave her a gift of money. She was going back to London, which she told me. Her father lives there, and she was longing to see him. I warned her about that man Bill Henry, but they say she went with him anyway, and look what come of it. If I'd have been there I might have stopped her." She shook her head sorrowfully.

"Is anyone *certain* that she went off with Bill Henry?" St. Ives asked her. "The *Gazette* reported that there were no witnesses."

"No sir, but Bill Henry talked to Daisy at the mill, and I heard him say that he would see her presently. I told the constable what I knew."

"You've brought the *Gazette* with you, I see," Mother Laswell said. "Is there more to the story now?"

"Not about Daisy," Clover told her. "There's this, which is why I was sent." She stepped across and handed a copy of the broadsheet to Mother Laswell along with the newspaper. She watched while the woman laid the broadsheet out onto a table and the five of them gathered round. They seemed to forget about Clover in the instant that they saw the photographs on the broadsheet, and at that juncture she turned away, nearly running into the blind girl. She came very near to whispering something hurtful to her, simply to put her in her place. But she was filled with the sense that the girl *saw* her, or saw *into* her, and she bolted into the kitchen and out through the door into the sunlight, hurrying away down the road.

She had surely heard enough to earn Henley's regard and perhaps another of his banknotes, which was certain, of course, if she gave him what else he wanted. The thought renewed her smile and she skipped along the grassy verge.

ALICE UNDERSTOOD THE nature of the broadsheet immediately: a piece of infamous slander. Across the top were the words "Witches Coven in Aylesford." Below that was an account of the coven's activities, which referred to "several women of note," although there were no names revealed. Whoever wrote the piece hadn't the fortitude to commit himself by being particular about names. Below that were photographs of the members of the Friends of the River Medway, taken at the soirée. There were others along with them, chosen randomly and also unnamed, as if the architect of the broadsheet wanted to avoid outright accusations.

There were three other photos, however, that were more troubling: unfortunately convincing frauds. One was of five women in filmy, transparent garments cavorting in a forest glade in the moonlight. Three of the women had their heads turned away, but two were looking forward. One had Alice's features and the other Mother Laswell's, although the woman with Mother Laswell's face wasn't quite stout enough to be convincing, nor was the Alice figure tall enough. Another photograph depicted what might be the same five women flying on brooms with long staffs through the night sky, dressed in black robes. Clara was among them, wearing her dark spectacles, and both Alice and Mother Laswell were clearly identifiable. Beneath it was the caption, 'Fly-by-nights.' A third showed the same five—or so it clearly implied—but Alice and Mother Laswell were the only two whose faces were clear. They were gathered in the moonlight that shone on the standing stones at Kit's Coty House. The Mother Laswell figure held a curved knife in her hand, her robes partly hiding a rickety altar made of sticks.

"What does he hope to accomplish with this outrage?" Alice asked, breaking the silence. "It's *evidently* false."

"They hope to compel you to deny it," St. Ives said, "merely to tarnish your good name."

"*They?*" Alice asked. "Surely this is the work of the small man at the soirée, the photographer who was so anxious to have our likenesses. Why would he have any interest in our *denying* something?"

"He has no interest in it at all," Mother Laswell said, collapsing backward into her chair. "He was paid to do this work, Alice."

"By whom? Who on earth would pay him to…? Do you mean this man Townover?"

"Surely not," Frobisher said. "It flies in the face of reason."

"It seems entirely reasonable to me, Mr. Frobisher," Mother Laswell said. "You've backed the wrong horse, I'm afraid, or come close to backing it."

"There must be a way of discovering who actually put the photographer up to it," Alice said. "Langdon, you told me that you had learned something of his whereabouts. I had no interest in the subject an hour ago, but I do now. I intend to confront the man."

"We both will," Mother Laswell said evenly. "We'll get some of the truth out of him. See if we don't."

"We'll go together," St. Ives said. "The railway porter informed me that he came up from Tunbridge Wells on the train, that he had a shop or a studio very near Dockett's Trunks and Cases—two doors down, he said. We can find him right enough."

"Look at this," Mother Laswell said, holding out the *Gazette* now. There was another photograph on the front page, this one of the soirée, showing the pasteboard paper mill going up in flames, with Mother Laswell and Bill Kraken standing alongside. *Anarchist gathering in Aylesford!* the headline shrieked. "It's all here," she said, reading the piece. "Not just the soirée, that's plain enough, but the past along with it, dug up like a skeleton out of the grave." She read further in silence, her eyes sweeping back and forth. "Here's the death of my first husband, retold—the fire that burnt him up, and the children's bodies they found buried beneath his laboratory. The murder of Sarah Wright follows. It names Harriet Laswell in each, which is fair enough when it comes to my husband, since he died by my hand. But that I was involved in Sarah's beheading…"

She dropped the paper and began to weep, putting her open hand to her forehead.

"But you were *exonerated*," Alice said to her. "You were never charged for the death of your husband. This hasn't been current for twenty-five years. Can they do this, Langdon?"

"Yes," he said. "It's intentionally ruinous, but there's nothing libelous or criminal in it. They've left that for the broadsheet, which they'll give away on the street and distribute to every public house in the area, with no one taking credit for producing it."

"I must admit that I'm puzzled," Frobisher said. "When you spoke to Charles Townover, Professor, did he know who you were?"

"I'm not certain. I'd met him some months back, but he made nothing of it. I told him, of course, that you and I are friends."

"I see. This...this scheme...," Frobisher said, "was clearly put into motion prior to this morning when you visited the mill. The ink is scarcely dry on the broadsheet, but it's dry enough for the thing to have been distributed. This photographer worked through the night to accomplish it, and with the aid of a newspaper to print copies—perhaps someone at the *Gazette* or at the newspaper office in Tunbridge Wells." It seemed almost as if Gilbert were talking to himself now, trying

to regenerate the enthusiasm he'd mustered only min-
utes ago. He stared at the floor for a time and then said,
"Who is the *perpetrator?* That's the mystery. Not Charles
Townover. No, sir. The man still believes I might invest.
It makes no sense at all that he would go to these lengths
to undermine..."

There was the sound of horse's hooves now, and
through the window St. Ives saw the children standing
with painted faces alongside the mule Ned Ludd, the lot
of them watching as Bill Kraken galloped away down the
lane in a cloud of dust.

Chapter 13

Murder in Tunbridge Wells

OCKETT'S TRUNKS AND CASES was known to Kraken. He had been to Tunbridge Wells a dozen times, had purchased sheep there, and had purchased the very horse he rode now, Old Bluenose, from a farmer another mile up the way toward Green Hill. He stood on Camden Road, across the street from Dockett's. The photographer's studio—Manfred Pink's—sat two buildings down. Its door was locked, and there were shutters over the windows.

Manfred *Pink*, Kraken thought. That was no sort of a name for a man. A man with such a name, who would do these things, wanted badly to be knocked on the head, and Kraken had half a mind to climb in through a window and…

That wouldn't be wise, though. Mother was always recommending wisdom. He wondered whether she had known where he was bound, him leaving like that, without a word, but if he'd said a word, he'd have said ten, and then what? Had they followed him? Three women passed along the pavement, and he nodded to them. They sidled into the street at the sight of him, however, and hastened away, looking back with obvious suspicion— something that was simply his lot in life, and he took no offense in it.

Now that the question of his being followed was hovering in his mind, it came to him that there was no time for idleness, and he crossed the road and went up between the buildings, where he found himself in a weedy yard with a wooden hovel beyond. There was a broad meadow behind the hovel and a woods in the distance. The door to the hovel was just then opening, and a small boy stepped out. He saw Kraken, a look of surprise crossed his face, and immediately he stepped back inside and shut the door. It was the boy who had been with Pink at the soirée. Kraken had no quarrel with him, but it was a rum thing, since the boy had known him.

He heard noise from within Pink's—a clattering and the sound of a cabinet door banging shut. So the villain was within, perhaps in a hurry, and yet the front door of his shop was locked at midday. Kraken glanced back at the hovel, but the boy had gone to ground. So be it.

He climbed the three wooden stairs to the porch and stood listening at the door, hearing the creak of the sign that read "Pink's" shifting overhead on its iron rings. He had the sudden urge to rip the sign from its moorings and smash it through the window, but he clapped a stopper over the compulsion, thinking of Mother Laswell again, how she had suffered, and how he mustn't be the cause for more. Steadier now, he put his hand on the metal knob, turning it silently. When it swung open he stepped through and shut the door behind him. There stood the small man, Manfred Pink, wearing his audacious hat and looking down at a photograph. Pink swung toward him, shouting out loud in surprise, his eyes widening, as if he saw his doom.

"You're a-going out, are you?" asked Kraken, noting that the man was wearing his coat and that there was a valise sitting on the floorboards several feet from the door. Kraken stepped to the valise, snatched it up, unlatched it and dumped it out onto the floor—shirts and small-clothes and a pair of shoes, followed by the thump of rolled banknotes, which Kraken stooped to pick up, saying, "Well, now! Where might *you* be..."

Instantly Pink leapt forward and dealt him a savage blow on the head, knocking him over a chair, a heavy glass paperweight flying out of his hand and banging down onto the floorboards. Kraken found himself entangled in chair-legs, blind from the blood pouring down out of his scalp. He heard Pink go out, slamming the door behind him as Kraken pushed himself to his feet. He stood reeling, bewildered by the blow. The contents of the valise still lay on the ground, although the banknotes were gone.

He saw now that there was a photograph, however, fallen half out of a pasteboard envelope and lying atop a nightshirt. He picked up both and used the shirt to wipe his bloody face. The photograph depicted a wooden table with a dead baby lying atop it, a long, bloody gash in its chest. Kraken dropped it in horror and then snatched it up again, thinking of what had been pictured in the broadsheet—the altar-like table that sat before the old standing stones. He slid the photograph into his shirt. What it meant, he couldn't say—filthy trash, that was clear—but it wouldn't do to leave it lying about.

Pink had got away without any comeuppance— certainly not far, however. He mopped his scalp again and stepped toward the door. As he reached for the knob the door smashed inward, knocking him backward. Pink staggered through it, making sounds in his throat. He turned, his eyes wide, and Kraken saw that both his hands clutched the handle of a heavy clasp knife, imbedded to the hilt in his chest. Pink lurched toward Kraken, apparently trying to speak through a bloody froth, and Kraken picked up the broken chair and fended him off, Pink falling onto his own scattered clothing and lying still.

It was past time to get out. Kraken looked hastily out the door, and, seeing no murderers lurking, he slipped through it and closed it behind him, realizing then that he still carried the bloody shirt that he'd mopped his face with. He pitched it into the weeds and hastened away, his mind working out how to get around to where he had tied up old Bluenose without making a spectacle of himself, as Mother would say. He meant simply ride Bluenose into the wood and find his way back to Hereafter roundaboutly.

He hoped to God that Mother was safe at home, and he wondered whether a lie would suffice to explain his head. But he saw quickly that it would *not* suffice, that he must tell her the truth and hope that she *saw* it was the truth, and not something else. She wouldn't argue with the photograph. He had been in luck to find it. It might serve to do the proving—Pink's having it—or it might mean damnation, in which case he would burn it in the garden.

Chapter 14

Father and Son

HENLEY WATCHED HIS FATHER'S face. The old man could not dissemble; he wasn't built for it. His face made plain what he thought, and he was evidently perplexed about something and angry into the bargain, although surely he could have no suspicion that the idiot Bill Henry was an innocent man.

"I've been contemplating on something, Henley," Townover said, leaning back in his chair and looking down his nose. "I asked you quite clearly to write out a draft for the Dumpel girl's money on the mill's account in Threadneedle Street. That would have compelled her to return to London. It would also make her relatively safe from thieves. Why did you not do as I asked?

You knew as well as I that this man Henry was lurking about and that the girl hadn't the sense to see him for what he was."

"I was pressed for time, father. It's as simple as that. The banknotes were handy and they amounted to the same thing. Davis was set to put her on the train, London bound. I couldn't have known the idiot girl would go off with Henry. And in any event, the money has come back to us."

Townover stared at him unhappily. "The money is immaterial to me. The girl's death is not. I believe that she was murdered for the money. Mere greed. A man of Henry's type wants motivation, and the banknotes supplied him with motivation aplenty. In our way we were responsible for Daisy's death. I was irritated with the girl, certainly, but this…" He shook his head and stared hard into his Henley's eyes. "I mean to say that to my mind, your *impatience* murdered the girl."

Henley mastered his feelings and then said, "Looking back now, I see my error. I admit it, and certainly I take full responsibility. But there's nothing to *see* if one looks back *before* anything untoward has happened."

"Perhaps. But consider that one day this mill might very well belong to you. It is easy for a man to say that he accepts full responsibility for his actions, but it's a phrase that comes easily into the mind when there are no real consequences. I adjure you to consider things more carefully before you act. Do this for the sake of the mill's good name if not for your own."

"I quite understand," Henley said, bowing. "I regret this very much, father." *Might very well belong to you.* Henley considered the implication of the phrasing. It was clearly a threat.

"Your apology, such as it is, will have to suffice, given that the girl is dead. I'm late for the meeting with Frobisher. He's supping at Windhover tonight. Will you join us?"

"Alas, I cannot, father. I wish I had known yesterday, before I made promises."

"If I had known yesterday, I would have informed you yesterday."

"Exactly." He looked steadily at his father, although he knew it was rash.

"Frobisher seems to be anxious to part with some of his money," Townover said after a heavy silence. "At least the man knows something about paper. Godfrey Pallinger had no notion of it, nor did the other prospect. Their only interest was in profit, which to my mind makes them tiresome objects. I'm keen to hear what Frobisher has to say."

"As am I," Henley said, as he watched his father don his coat and top-hat before the old man went out through the office door and descended the stairs. Alone now, Henley stood up and walked to the window where he looked out at the darkening river, the evening sunlight dwindling as night fell. Had the old man seen something in the very *fact* of the banknotes that had raised his suspicions? That scarcely seemed possible. Certainly his father must see the banknotes as a blunder and nothing more. He thought of what Davis had told him of his father's meeting with the meddlesome St. Ives earlier in the day, however, and of St. Ives's visit to the Malden Arms. Thank God Davis had kept that fact a secret. Henley could discredit the rest of his enemies—had already done so—but his father was a different matter entirely. Perhaps the old man would choke to death on a chicken bone this evening and simplify everything a hundredfold.

He returned to the desk, where he sat in his father's chair, his mind working until Davis entered the room. "Clover's hoping to come up," Davis said. "She was waiting for Mr. Townover to leave before she showed herself."

Henley nodded. "What about Pink? Is it done?"

"Jenks saw to him."

"You're certain?"

"Dead certain. There was a man in Pink's office—the husband of the Laswell woman, Bill Kraken."

"You astonish me. In Pink's *office?*"

"Pink was running from him, scared like, and carrying a bag, like he was leaving for good and all. Jenks put a knife into Pink after he come out and then pushed him back into the office, which is how he knew Kraken was there. Pink had bashed Kraken on the head, and he was running blood. Jenks left quick, thinking that Kraken could take the blame."

"Jenks is sure that Kraken didn't see him?"

"Jenks says no. Any gait, Jenks was wearing a balaclava, so it makes no difference."

Henley considered it, then laughed out loud. "*Kraken!* The stupid fool. I wonder what put him onto Pink. That was fast work."

"It could be Clover knows. Will I send her up?"

"Yes, but what about the 500 pounds that was paid to Pink for the photographs? Did Jenks recover it? If Pink was running, surely he had the money on his person."

Davis shook his head. "Not yet, sir."

"Not *yet?*"

"Jenks looked into Pink's bag, which he'd dropped outside, but the money weren't in it, and he couldn't search Pink's office with Kraken still inside. There was no time. Jenks had to scarper. No doubt Pink has it hid. Jenks says he'll go back to look when it's safe."

"Does he indeed? Why would Pink have hidden such a large sum if he intended to flee at the first opportunity?"

Davis shrugged. "There's something in that, sure."

"Would Jenks keep the money for himself, do you suppose, if he found it?"

"If he saw his main chance and thought he'd get away with it. Lots of men would keep it and call it a bit of luck."

"Indeed they would," Henley said. He sat looking out the window at the evening sky for a moment while Davis waited. "I want you to find out the truth. Let us assume that Jenks found it and kept it. Tell Jenks what you just said to me—that it was a bit of luck. Tell him that you'd like to share in the luck. One hundred pounds should do it. You don't need a *full* share, given it was Jenks who did the work. Tell him that you convinced me that the money was lost. Any sort of lie that will serve. If Jenks gives you the hundred pounds, show it to me. It behooves both of us to know whether we can trust the man."

"There's truth in that. I'll see him tonight, and put it to him like you said."

"Good. You have another thing or two to accomplish tonight, I believe. I don't have to tell you that if you're seen at Hereafter Farm, it could mean ruin."

Davis nodded.

"Then send Clover up, if you will, and leave us alone. We're not to be disturbed."

Suppressing a grin, Davis turned toward the door.

"And, Davis…" Henley said.

"Sir?"

"You and Jenks can have Clover when she's served her purpose. Or perhaps you alone if Jenks isn't hanging about."

Davis nodded and went out, and Clover entered directly, evidently full of news. She had grown bold, it seemed to Henley. But the forward, cunning look on her face brought out her beauty, or something that passed for it.

"What did you discover at Hereafter Farm?" he asked her. "You delivered the broadsheet, I trust."

"Well, sir, I took the papers to the farm as you said, and didn't their eyes *shoot* open when they saw them."

"Who, Clover? *Who* saw them?"

"Why the one they call Mother Laswell, and also the St. Ives woman and her man. And Mother Laswell's husband, it must have been. You'd best watch out for him. He's a fire-brand, that one is. And Mr. Frobisher was with them, talking a blue streak about what he meant to do. I left them to it and went off, and I was half a mile down the lane when I heard a horse coming up, and so I stepped into a copse and hid. It was the husband. He was in a wild state for certain—on a desperate mission, I thought."

"Do you know where he was bound?"

"No, sir."

"And that's the lot of it then? You knocked upon the door and handed Mother Laswell the broadsheet and the *Gazette*, watched her eyes *shoot open*, and walked away?"

"Oh, no sir," she said, smiling coyly at him. "Aren't *you* in a state, sir? I didn't knock upon the door at all. I saw there was no one about, and so I walked in as bold as Jack Straw and listened from the hallway. Do you wish to know what I heard, perhaps?"

"Of course I do, Clover. You know it full well."

"And will you be good to me?"

"As good as ever I can be."

She smiled broadly, hiked her skirts, sat down atop the desk, and with Henley's hand upon her knee, she told him what she had heard.

Chapter 15

Suspicions

W HAT A SHAMBLES OF a day," Alice said, sitting on the edge of the bed and knotting her hair. The candles guttered in the night breeze, which was exotically warm. She looked closely at St. Ives and whispered, "And now we discover that our island harbors a coven of witches!"

"I'm quite fond of those witches, so I see it as a general improvement."

"But what should the witches do about it?"

"About my being fond of them?" he asked. "I'm particularly fond of *one* of them, actually. As for doing something about it…" He smiled at her and received a smile in return.

"Perhaps we'll get to that," she said. "Should we *answer* the charges, though? Should we say anything at all? The entire thing is the work of a small, disturbed mind."

"I counsel silence. It could be that the mind that conceived the thing isn't as small as it would seem. More to the point, small minds and small ambitions can be dangerous things. He evidently commissioned the photographs some time ago. Such necessities aren't left until the last moment. Mother Laswell hasn't kept her mission a secret, after all."

"*He?* How do you know it's a man?"

"Women are largely above this sort of thing. There's a salacious quality to the deviousness that reveals a man's mind."

"And Charles Townover is *not* the man? You seem very sure of that, as does Gilbert."

"I'm sure of nothing," St. Ives said. "Townover is quite capable of sending Daisy away. She was sick, and a liability to the mill. But I believe that he paid her what he thought was a sufficient sum for her troubles. He intended to send her off to London, just as he asserts. She might in fact have recovered, once she was no longer breathing the poisons."

"I would agree but for the fact that Daisy had been attending the Friends gatherings. She was a potential threat to the mill and not merely a sick girl."

"You're correct, of course. When I met with Townover we were interrupted by the mill foreman, a man named Davis. Hasbro and I had run into Davis, almost literally, when we were gathering samples along the river. I'm quite sure that he saw my face that night, and from the look on his own face this morning, I could see that he knew me. And yet he denied it. We both knew it was a lie, but I cannot fathom the reason for the lie. When Davis attacked us along the brook he was merely doing his duty. He can have no liking for me. It would have been sensible for him to reveal my activities to Townover on the spot, and to have me pitched out."

Alice sat down on the bed and leaned back against the headboard now. "Was Townover aware of the lie?" she asked.

"I believe not, although there's no certainty. Davis followed me across the river to Snodland, however, and looked into the Malden Arms, where I was breakfasting. He ascertained that I was there and then went away. So he has his eye on me."

"And yet you don't suspect Townover's hand behind this?"

"Not behind all of it, no. I agree with Gilbert there. Davis would have been aware that Daisy was carrying a sum of money. If the demise of both Bill Henry and Daisy Dumpel was contrived by Davis, as it well might have been, then Davis is the culprit. Certainly he has a criminal air about him. It was Davis who provided evidence against Henry, and it was Davis who beat him senseless in the alley behind the Malden Arms and could quite easily have slipped Daisy's banknotes into Henry's coat."

"Daisy would have been an easy mark," Alice said. "She believed that Davis was looking after her. What if it was he and not Bill Henry who collected her from the Chequers? According to the *Gazette*, no one saw the man come in or got a look at him going out. But then what's to be gained by Davis? He had his hands on one hundred pounds and he gave it away in order to implicate Henry."

"He stands to gain something more than one hundred pounds, perhaps. It seemed to me that Townover's gift to Daisy was at least partly intended to buy her silence. But what if someone wanted to buy a more permanent silence? Perhaps Davis is another pawn."

"Or merely a murderer who is in the habit of taking what he wants."

"Possibly."

They lay there in silence for a time, and then Alice said, "There's no proof of any of this, and Bill Henry and Daisy are both dead. You don't intend to pursue it, I hope, unless there's something more certain. And then you'd be wise to go to Constable Brooke. He's a good man."

"As you will."

"And it could be that all of this is finished, you know. The Friends of the Medway are discredited. Bill Henry and Daisy are silenced. It seems to be a thorough-going success."

"I very much hope you're right," St. Ives said.

And then they blew out their candles and settled in for the night.

Chapter 16

It Looks Like Witches

S T. IVES SAT ON the veranda the next morning, recalling his conversation with Alice. There was nothing he could think of to do about this mess. The more one protested, the deeper one sank into the mire, and yet it seemed to him that there must be some relevant action—that a plot had been hatched, and that the chick was growing into a chicken.

He smiled at the figure. Perhaps Alice was correct. The Friends of the Medway had been discredited. The damage was done. They would survive it, although Mother Laswell would scarcely lay down her cudgels, nor should she. Perhaps Gilbert would succeed and the chicken sent packing.

Eddie ran up onto the porch now. "Larkin wants to know can we take the rubber off the arrows," he said, "and sharpen them. We mean to shoot at a hay bale. She's made a target. A great giant rat. Ten points if you pierce its eye and five through the heart."

St. Ives considered the notion. Eddie was a sensible boy; his sister Cleo was flighty, but not foolish. Larkin was outright wild, but her heart was right and she had wonderful, arcane skills, many of which might someday lead her to the gallows. "Where will you position the hay bale, then?"

"Against the far wall of the barn, near the capstan. We've been feeding sugar-canes to Dr. Johnson, and he wants to observe the shooting."

"Nowhere near the balloon, though? And Dr. Johnson must be well clear. Shooting an arrow anywhere near a balloon or an elephant isn't to be countenanced. Not for a moment."

"Oh, no sir," Eddie said. "Yes, sir, I mean. None of us would count...do what you said."

"And you'll draw a line that must be stood behind."

"Yes, sir."

"And there will be no notched arrows when someone is collecting the spent arrows. Do I make myself clear?"

"Yes, sir. Just as you say."

"And do not allow Johnson to eat all of his sugar canes at one sitting. He must be content with two or three, like you or I or the next fellow. They won't be replenished until the end of the week. It's a kindness to him to parse them out."

"Yes, sir," Eddie said, and then before there could be any more admonitions, he bolted toward the barn, hollering something that St. Ives couldn't make out. He was distracted by the sight of Constable Brooke stepping down from his buggy at the end of the wisteria alley. St. Ives went out to meet him, deadly certain that something further was amiss, that the island was under siege.

"Is Mrs. St. Ives at home, sir?" Brooke asked after the two men had shaken hands.

"Upstairs, yes. I'm afraid she's slept late. Shall I awaken her?"

"Might I speak to you first?"

"Of course, Brooke. Come, take a chair on the porch."

The two men ascended the porch steps into the shade and sat down. "I don't like to be here at all, sir. Not on such a day as this," Brooke said.

"I see. State your mind freely," St. Ives told him. "I half expected you'd pay us a visit sooner or later."

"It's not good news sir, and to my mind it's dead wrong, but I must do my duty by the constabulary."

"Of course you must."

"Bill Kraken's been taken up for murder, do you see? It appears as if he's killed a man named Manfred Pink, a photographer fellow from Tunbridge Wells. He and Pink had some sort of falling out, and Kraken murdered him with a clasp knife—a single blow, in the heart."

St. Ives stood in shocked silence. It was certainly possible that Kraken had done just this thing—horribly possible. Kraken was impetuous, and he had ridden off in a state yesterday. "Were there witnesses?"

"No, sir. Pink's body was found, and there was a hue and cry. Kraken was riding toward Aylesford from Tunbridge Wells when he was brought to bay by three citizens. Pink had struck him on the head—Kraken admits as much—but he denied having touched Pink. It wasn't his knife, he said, but that of an unseen hand, as they say. When he was captured he had a photograph concealed on his person, however—a dead baby slit open by a knife and bleeding out."

"Which he had taken from Pink's, no doubt, as I would have done if I had seen it there. Have you seen the infamous broadsheet, Brooke?"

"Yes, sir, I have."

"And you're aware that the photographs are frauds?"

"Truth to tell, I don't know what's frauds, sir. And what I know, or what I think, makes little difference. I haven't got to the end of what I came to say, neither."

"Tell me the lot of it, then. We'll sort it out."

"It ain't the sort of thing that can be sorted, Professor, but here it is. After Kraken was jailed, we went out to

Hereafter to see Mother Laswell, naturally, and what did we find but the table made of sticks that was on the broadsheet you mentioned—a satanic altar, so they say. It stood behind the barn under a bit of canvas, and there was blood on the table-top and a bloody knife underneath along with a jar of…" He looked down at the ground now and muttered, "…what they call flying ointment."

St. Ives burst into laughter. "I won't pretend not to understand you, Brooke, but for the love of God how does anyone know what was contained within the jar? Did it have a *label* on it, as if it had come from the chemist's?"

"In fact it did, sir—that very thing. But like I was saying, out we went to Kit's Coty, and found the dead baby itself buried on the meadow near the old stones, the same baby as was in the photograph that Kraken took from Pink's."

St. Ives looked away, forcing himself to breathe evenly. "Was the photo of the dead baby taken from afar, so to speak?"

"No sir, near-on."

"How can that be? It would mean that between the baby's being killed—if in fact it *was* killed—and the time it was buried, Pink managed to take a photograph of it. How was this done? Did this alleged coven of witches, which I remind you seems to include my wife, *invite* Pink to take such a photograph, one which would damn them for good and all? It doesn't stand to reason, man."

Constable Brook shrugged. "That will surely come out, sir, but at the moment it's evidence."

"And the dead baby. Where was it removed to?"

"Dr. Pullman has it."

"Good. Was Mother Laswell arrested, then?"

"There was an attempt, but she beat one of the men with a twig broom and ran into the woods. We searched, but she'd hid herself."

"Good again, by God. She's an innocent woman. Did you confiscate the broom? Perhaps it's the very broom that she rides upon—another piece of evidence."

Brooke blinked at him. "I didn't think to…"

"Fetch it, man. If Dr. Pullman can find traces of flying ointment on the staff, then you've got your woman dead to rights. Did you think of that?" St. Ives realized that he was very near to breaking out. He didn't want to savage Brooke, who was a kind if unimaginative man, but he badly wanted to savage something. He reined himself in, however, forcing himself to compose his face.

"What else, then?" he asked.

Brooke stared at him, his mouth half open. "Only I've come to arrest Mrs. St. Ives. It's her picture with the witches, you see. She's implicated."

"There *are* no witches, Brooke."

"Maybe not, sir. I hope not. But it *looks* like witches. And there's the stones at Kit's Coty and the bloody altar and the baby and Pink murdered, and two bloody knives alongside all. We don't quite know where to start. We've got to…"

"Witchcraft hasn't been a punishable offense for 150 years, Brooke. Surely you're aware of that."

He shrugged unhappily. "There's a murdered baby, sir, no matter was it witchcraft or not."

From somewhere behind them, hidden in the shadows of the porch, Alice said, "I'll come along peacefully, Constable Brooke." She'd apparently been standing inside the door, listening. "As Langdon said, we'll sort this out. I'll just be a few minutes getting some things together."

Alice left, and the two men stood in silence. St. Ives's mind was swimming helplessly, but he saw nothing solid to clutch on to. "Tell me, Brooke, was Clara Wright arrested? Surely you do not believe that a blind girl was riding atop a broom."

"No sir. Only your Alice and Mother Laswell, who were at Kit's Coty. Their faces were plain."

"They were *not* at Kit's Coty, Brooke. The photograph is a fraud."

"Yes, sir. No doubt it is, but…"

Mrs. Langley stepped out onto the porch now with two glasses of lemonade. Gilbert Frobisher was with her.

"My throat is closed," St. Ives said, waving his glass away. Brooke, who was in the act of reaching for one of the glasses, hesitated.

"This will open your throat, sir. Mrs. St. Ives said that I must make an offer of lemonade and that's what I'm a-doing. Take your glass, Constable."

Brooke nodded and did as he was told, as did St. Ives, both men drinking it straight down. Brooke looked away, as if studying the wisteria alley, and Mrs. Langley went back inside with the empty glasses.

St. Ives could think of nothing to say, but his mind was working now. It seemed clear to him that everything he had imagined about the man Davis was true. But it still seemed unlikely that Davis could be the linch-pin. He was a mere hireling, and had nothing to gain by fabricating ornate plots. Someone else meant to gain by it.

"A word with you, Constable?" Frobisher asked, and Brooke nodded with a look of apparent relief on his face. The two men walked off, Gilbert speaking, and a moment later St. Ives observed his friend handing Brooke several banknotes.

Alice and Mrs. Langley came out through the door, Alice carrying her portmanteau, which St. Ives took from her.

"Do you want the children?" Mrs. Langley asked her.

"Yes," Alice answered. "What I do not want are secrets, although we'd best wait until after I've gone to make things particularly clear, whatever that means." Mrs. Langley hurried away toward the barn.

"You'll consider your actions carefully, won't you, Langdon?" Alice asked, looking into his eyes. "Nothing rash. Anger never helps. It always rebounds upon a person."

"Yes," he said. "You're right, of course."

"Do you know, I've never been happier that there are two of us."

He nodded, but said, "Did you hear the entire conversation? It's difficult to generate anything like happiness."

"I did hear it. But I choose to be happy that we're husband and wife. I suggest that you contact Mr. Bayhew so that he can find a barrister in the event that there is to be a trial. A clever lawyer will destroy them, whoever they are."

"Yes, of course. I'll send to Bayhew immediately." He hadn't thought to do so, despite their long friendship with Bayhew, who had acted as their solicitor several times in the past. Alice kissed him now, which surprised him, although he kissed her back heartily enough. They walked to where Brooke and Frobisher were apparently contemplating the hops field, their conversation at an end. "Is Alice to be taken to the jail in Aylesford?" St. Ives asked Brooke.

"No, sir. It's taken up by Bill Kraken," Brooke said. "If we can find Mother Laswell, she can join Bill, of course, the two of them together."

"Maidstone, then?"

He shook his head. "To Snodland, sir, which is sitting empty since Bill Henry went and…and it's somewhat nicer, ma'am—more spacious. There's a view of the ferry landing through the window, the people coming and going, which no doubt…" He stopped speaking, crossed his arms, and looked at his feet.

"I've given the constable the means to see to Alice's comfort," Gilbert whispered to St. Ives, but before St. Ives could respond, Mrs. Langley and the children—Finn Conrad and Larkin along with Eddie and Cleo—were coming along from the barn. Mrs. Langley had said something to the children, because they were uncharacteristically quiet and serious. Larkin gave Brooke a hard stare when they drew near, and Cleo burst into tears.

"I told them that you were going off for a day or two, ma'am," Mrs. Langley said.

Alice kissed each of them on the cheek, including Finn. "I'll be home quite soon," she said, then smiled convincingly and turned away. It wasn't difficult to see that she was weeping, and Cleo cried all the harder. St.

Ives and Mrs. Langley pinned the children when Alice and Constable Brooke walked toward the buggy in the wisteria alley.

"We'll serve the copper out, see if we don't," Larkin said to Eddie in a low voice.

"We'll have no talk of serving anyone out, Larkin," Frobisher said to her. "Constable Brooke is doing what he must do. We'll turn this entire business into a laughing matter in short order, as my old dad said before they pulled the trap." He uttered a short laugh, but cut it off, as if realizing that perhaps it wasn't quite appropriate.

St. Ives watched until Alice was out of sight, the very idea of laughing seeming outrageous, and as they trudged silently back toward the house he considered what it was he would say to the children.

Chapter 17

At Breakfast

A T WINDHOVER, YES," GILBERT Frobisher said across the breakfast table next morning. "Townover possesses quite an acreage, but left wild for the hunting. He has no interest in growing crops, although he has a prodigious number of sheep, apparently. His gamekeeper was complaining of poachers when I was shown in, and Charles spoke of the merits of public hangings. I was never fond of hangings."

Frobisher, St. Ives, and Hasbro sat over the remains of breakfast, although St. Ives had scarcely eaten. Frobisher had acquitted himself well, however, and was helping himself to more rashers and toast. "He's a hard man, is Charles, although he had an ancient dog sitting at his feet the entire time. He clearly had an enormous affection for it. He's not without sentiment, I mean to say.

I remain satisfied that he knows nothing of these cowardly machinations. If he's responsible for any of it, he's both a madman and a consummate actor."

"I wasn't aware that he had a son," St. Ives said. "It's unfortunate that the son wasn't there so that you could have had a look at him."

"The son—Henley—stands to inherit," Frobisher said, "but he currently owns no shares in the mill. Charles is in complete control, legally speaking. His decision to sell direct shares is recent, apparently, perhaps to do with his health. He rejected the other investors because they were intent on having a controlling interest rather than being mere speculators, and because they were overly eager to talk about dividends. They wanted guarantees. Charles is considering my offer only because of the specifics of it. Our contract would necessarily cede me limited control in carefully defined areas. I listed them succinctly on a sheet of foolscap, keeping Mother Laswell's concerns in mind, of course, and signed my name to it. I made it clear that my offer was complete and final, that I did not intend to invest without assurances. I made no mention of dividends or guarantees. To the contrary, I meant to put my own money into solving the mill's troubles, such as they were."

"Given the nature of your discussion, I wonder that the son wasn't on hand," Hasbro said. "It seems to me that he would have an avid interest in the business, given that it will some day be his own. How old a man is Charles Townover?"

"Very nearly my own age, sixty-six or seven."

"What's the nature of his illness?"

"His heart seizes, apparently," St. Ives said. "Alice and I met him at a function when he was newly arrived in Kent, although he mightn't remember it. He carried a vial of physic."

"He swilled the stuff when I visited the mill," Gilbert said. "He was apoplectic when a girl spoke out of turn—a furious passion, really. He knew, it, however, and uncorked his vial."

"Does the son Henley live at Windhover?" Hasbro asked.

"Apparently," Frobisher said. "And he's very much involved in the running of the mill. Charles has a high regard for his abilities. It would be Henley who would help carry out the changes that I proposed, apparently. Charles regretted that his son wasn't at home, although to my mind it wasn't altogether strange. He could have had no notion of my proposition, and Charles had already sent the two other investors packing. A young man like Henley would no doubt have better things to do than to listen to old men talk."

Mrs. Langley entered, carrying a basket, the contents wrapped in a cloth. There were newspaper-wrapped parcels along with it. "I've put up something to eat, gentlemen. The basket is for poor Bill. The others are for the three of you—sandwiches made up out of last night's roast, with mustard. It'll be a long day, perhaps, with all the troubles descending."

Frobisher looked at his pocket watch. "And it's already drawing on. Finn Conrad has promised to show me the resident birds this morning, so I'm off. I won't be far afield, however. Townover promised to send a reply this very afternoon."

"And I'm bound for Tunbridge Wells," St. Ives said. "Will you give my best wishes to Bill Kraken, Hasbro? Speak to him privately if ever you can."

"Brooke will allow it, I believe. Perhaps Bill has some notion of where Mother Laswell has gone to ground. If he has, I'll look out for her upon my return."

"We'll rendezvous at four o'clock, then?" St. Ives said. "God willing we'll have discovered something that will cast a light on all this darkness."

Chapter 18

Roast Beef with Mustard

RIDING ALICE'S HORSE PENNYLEGS, a name provided by Cleo when she was three years old, St. Ives entered Tunbridge Wells from the northeast along a disused track that had taken him through a long stretch of empty woods. On any other day he would have been on the lookout for mushrooms and low areas of marsh where he might find something interesting crawling along the bank of a pond, but today he was almost indifferent to these things, including a particularly clear-running chalk stream that was unknown to him. His sole intention was to avoid being seen.

He rode out onto a broad, sheep-populated meadow now, seeing the back lots of buildings along the eastern edge of Tunbridge Wells, one of which would be Pink's, if in fact it were as near to Dockett's as Jeffries the porter had recalled. He had no desire to be recognized or challenged, but he fully intended to have a look inside Pink's shop, and he had brought along a packet of bent wires and skeleton keys that might prove useful.

He saw Pink's sign now, above the rear door of a shop, and he dismounted and tied Pennylegs to a post. There were people about, although somewhat far off, and so he made no effort to be furtive. A tumbledown shack stood some distance away, the door slightly ajar. He would give it a quick look in due time. As for now, he contemplated the iron lock fixed to the door—a warded lock that was quite new, although it hadn't helped Pink avoid his fate. The man had apparently been playing for dangerously high stakes. Or, he thought, it was possible that the police had put the lock on the door to secure the place, in which case he had best be quick about it. He withdrew the ring of skeleton keys and tried two before the third unlocked it. He pushed the door open, stepped inside, and closed it again.

He had a look into the darkroom, suspecting that he would find nothing useful. There were glass photographic plates aplenty, but the images on them were of no consequence—weddings, funerals, and several photographs of dead children in lifelike poses. Death photographs had always seemed both sad and awful to him, but right now they were evidence of nothing. He came across a dozen plates with images taken at the soirée, but, again, they weren't evidence; it would be odd if there were not such images. Shards of broken glass plates lay scattered on the floor, as if, perhaps, Pink had hurriedly sought to destroy the evidence of his photographic chicanery or else had been frantically searching for particular plates. St. Ives studied pieces of them, and found what appeared to be a double image on one—one image laid over the top of the other—but it was a mere fragment of a picture. It showed that Pink had been experimenting with images, but it wasn't enough to clear Alice's name. He wondered what had been taken or destroyed—by Pink, by the men who had murdered Pink, by the police…

There were heavy bottles of chemicals, the most interesting being potassium cyanide, but Pink wasn't alleged to have been a poisoner: all of the chemicals were in keeping with his trade. There was a broad pool of dried blood on the floor of the office, and there were odd pieces of clothing tossed about, some of them blood-spattered. A broken chair lay in the corner, evidence, perhaps, of Kraken's battle with Pink, if indeed they had battled. There was no knowing what had gone on, except that it had been uncommonly bloody.

He opened the door again and stepped out, closing it behind him and locking it. Sixty feet away stood the tumbledown shack, the roof of which was collapsed at one corner, the boards along the mud-sill rotted and cracked, and the entire structure leaning precariously. The door was closed now. The wind? Someone lurking inside? There was a window looking out, with half the panes broken and with a ragged drape hung across. The place was evidently abandoned, and it was unlikely that Pink used it for storage in its ruined state—no evidence that it even belonged to him.

Now the drape moved in the wind, and, as it shifted aside, a boy's face was visible for a moment and then was covered again.

St. Ives set out at once toward the shack, trying the door but finding it locked, then going up alongside through the weedy lot, close to the tilted wall. He rounded the corner at the rear just as the boy was crawling out through a narrow hole made by two broken slats in the far corner. He saw St. Ives and pushed through in a panic, but was brought up short when his shirt caught on a jagged bit of wood. St. Ives collared him, seeing straightaway that he was Pink's lad. The boy struggled for another few seconds before giving up.

"Why do you mind *me?*" he asked, now that his shirt was free and he was on his feet. "I ain't done nothing. I worked for Pink, and that's all, hauling and such. I'm glad he's dead."

"The porter in Aylesford, on the station platform, said that Pink kicked you. Is that true?"

"True enough, and worse'n that." He sat down in a slump in the dirt, the fight gone out of him. He was thin, with a gaunt face and hollow cheeks, and he stared into the distance now. "They scragged old Pink, though. He got his." He nodded, continuing to stare, perhaps replaying Pink's downfall in his head.

"Did you see it, then?" St. Ives asked. "Was it a tall, thin man, with windy hair who stabbed him? He was…"

"No, it weren't him who did it. It was another man, short like, and wearing a hood so that you couldn't see his face."

"A broad man, then? Strong?" asked St. Ives, picturing the man whom Hasbro had brought down along the Eccles Brook three nights past—Davis's companion.

The boy nodded.

"Where was the tall, thin one? He's a friend of mine, you see, and he'll surely hang for the crime if we can't find the man in the hood."

"The man who burnt the town, you mean. He's your friend?"

"Burnt the town…? Of course! Yes, the man who burnt the town!"

"He went into Pink's, as you did just now, and then Mr. Pink came out a-running, and the other man in the hood came around the side and chased him, and Mr. Pink turned back and dodged him, trying for the door again, to save himself, and that's when the man put a knife in him. He dragged Mr. Pink up the steps and flung him inside again. I seen it from the window. The short man went off. And then out comes your tall man, all bloody like, and off he went in a hurry. Mr. Pink never again came out. The coppers was there later, but I went out through the hole and hid."

"You didn't speak to the police?"

"My old dad told me not to. Never. There's naught but trouble in it, no matter who you are."

St. Ives stared toward the distant woods, thinking this through. He was suddenly anxious to be away, but clearly he had to take the boy with him. "What is your name, then?"

"Willum, they call me."

"Do you fancy something to eat, Willum? I've brought sandwiches along—roast beef and mustard."

He shrugged.

"If you'll wait for me here, I'll fetch them. Are you living here, then? In the shanty?"

He shrugged again. "Mayhaps I am," he said.

"Wait for me," St. Ives said, and he ran to where Pennylegs was standing patiently and removed the lunch that Mrs. Langley had put up from the saddlebag. When he returned, the boy was sitting as he had been, and he took the proffered sandwich from St. Ives and set in on it, eating breathlessly. St. Ives left him to it, and in short order the food was gone. "I've another," St. Ives said, "but you should perhaps let the first slide down your gullet before you pitch another one after it. How long have you worked for Pink?"

"Since winter."

"Living here?"

"Where else am I to live? When I did a spot of work for Pink, he'd pay me a shilling."

"No more shillings now?"

He shrugged yet again, and St. Ives drew four shillings from his pocket and held them out in his open palm. The boy looked suspiciously into his face, but took the coins and held them in his fist.

"Will you go along with me? To save my friend from hanging?"

"Where to?"

"To a better life, I believe. The farm where they burned the pasteboard town. Hereafter, the farm is called. They'll take you in. You'll have to tell what you saw, though."

The boy nodded and stood up, and the two of them walked toward Pennylegs, but before they arrived, a constable rounded the corner and started toward Pink's door, a key in his hand. He looked up, saw St. Ives and Willum, and changed course, heading toward them now. Willum ran, down along the back of the buildings and around a corner, heading into the town proper. The constable gave chase, running hard when he passed St. Ives, but he was a stout man, easily past fifty years old, and he soon gave up the chase. His chest was heaving when he returned, and St. Ives waited for him to speak.

"State your business, if you please, sir," the constable said finally.

"I'm looking for the photographer, Manfred Pink. His shop seems to be locked up."

"You have business with Pink, then?"

"I do, sir. We paid him for work that he's yet to deliver."

"And he won't, neither. It's your bad luck, because Pink is dead—murdered. That was Pink's helpmate you were speaking to."

"Was it? He told me that he was an orphan, and I gave him four shillings."

"It simply encourages them, sir. You meant well, but now that Pink is dead, the boy has no business here."

"Perhaps the four shillings will help him on his way. Do you know how I can get hold of the photographs that are rightly mine? Pink might be dead, but he was paid for the work, and so they belong to me."

"Pink's is locked and his wares confiscated, at least for the moment—evidence, you know. You can file a claim at the constabulary on Slade Street. Do you know it?"

"I can find it. Thank you, officer. Good day to you now."

St. Ives walked to where Pennylegs waited and swung into the saddle, tipping his hat to the constable, who watched him ride away. He turned up along the alley where Willum had disappeared and followed it north along Camden Road until he left the town behind. He turned back toward the woods then, in order to return to Aylesford the same way he'd come. He ambled along, however, now and then looking behind him. He had crossed the meadow and was at the verge of the woods when he saw Willum following, his head nodding along behind tall grass in the distance.

He waited to allow the boy to catch up to him, but quickly lost sight of him. He ate the remaining sandwich, drank a bottle of ale, and listened to the flies buzzing in the lazy sunshine. A kestrel hovered over the meadow, and then swooped down and snatched up a small animal, too distant for St. Ives to identify it, a mole, perhaps. There was no sign of Willum, but it seemed odd that the boy would simply have been strolling across the meadow.

St. Ives turned Pennylegs toward the woods and rode along for a quarter mile before reining up again and moving into a small glade within sight of the path. He waited there in the shade for the boy to come along. Perhaps he was merely shy. Perhaps his flight from the constable had confounded whatever decision he had made earlier.

The waiting was futile. The afternoon was dragging on. He left the glade and set out in earnest for home at a leisurely pace, calculated to get him there in time for the rendezvous. He would have to put off his visit to Snodland until the evening. He admitted to himself that he had lost the boy, and in so doing had lost his chance to free Kraken and to prove that Pink was a part of a larger plot. Brooke would believe his story, of course: he and Brooke knew each other well enough. But a second-hand tale amounted to nearly nothing in a court of law.

Chapter 19

Lurking in the Kitchen

S T. IVES LAY ALONE in bed, a state that he was no longer used to. He thought of what Alice had told him—that she had never been happier that they were husband and wife, but that simply made her absence all the more sorrowful. When he and Hasbro had gone into Snodland that evening, he'd been happy to discover that Alice was comfortable in her cell. It had a window in it, albeit a barred window, and the room itself was large enough, with an iron bed rather than a cot. She had eaten a plate of food from the Malden Arms, "the stout gentleman, Mr. Frobisher, having put up a sum to pay the reckoning," as he had been told by the jailer.

But all was not well. A handbill, the ink still damp, had been distributed near the river, crying up the charges of witchcraft and with a photo of the dead baby. It called for the people of Snodland to take action, since the police were not doing so, but were feeding the perpetrators beef pies and mugs of porter at the expense of the citizenry. Eggs and tomatoes had been thrown at Alice's window, and a milling crowd had been routed by two constables, one of the officers taking a knock on the head from a bottle. Hasbro had elected to remain, standing guard in the road, just outside the window. He carried a rifle, but was under orders to fire the rifle only into the sky unless he was pushed to defend himself. When St. Ives had set out for home the environs of the jail had been peaceful.

He heard the children speaking in loud whispers on the sleeping porch. They had been uncharacteristically serious throughout the evening, although for the most obvious reason. They had overheard him telling Mrs. Langley what he had found in Snodland, and that Hasbro had remained. He hadn't meant for the children to hear, but he had not considered Larkin, who was too enterprising and attentive by half. He had seen them come out of Finn's cottage after nightfall, followed by Hodge the cat, Finn calling them back to say some final thing to them.

Something was afoot. Eddie and Cleo had become part of Larkin's gang, perhaps. Perhaps they had drafted Finn into the gang. No one had been forthcoming when he had asked them outright what they were up to, which was tantamount to mutiny. Cleo had begun to cry and said that she wanted her mother returned to them, and St. Ives had been hard pressed to hold back his own tears. He had tucked them up in bed over an hour ago, and he didn't have the heart to go downstairs to quiet them now. He was as addled as they were, after all, and he could scarcely require them to forget their troubles and keep mum.

Some time later he awakened from a dream, not knowing quite where he was and panicking suddenly when he sleepily discovered that Alice was missing. He heard the children again, their voices raised now, and his mind cleared. He slid out of bed and looked out onto the moonlit yard where, to his astonishment, Larkin was running down a fleeing boy like a hound running down a fox. Eddie and Cleo trailed along behind, their night-clothes flapping. It was Willum, the boy from Pink's, whom Larkin was chasing.

St. Ives's heart rose at the sight of him. Larkin, who wasn't much taller than five-year-old Cleo, pitched herself into the air and brought Willum down. Without pause, she scrambled onto his back and pressed him to the grass with her knees, grasping both his ears so that he couldn't turn his head. Eddie and Cleo caught up and stood over them.

St. Ives took the stairs two at a time, holding onto his nightcap, hurtling out through the door and down the several steps to the lawn, arriving in time to prevent Larkin from pummeling the boy across the back of the head more than once or twice.

"He had *this* in his pocket, sir!" Larkin said, holding up a watch on a fob. "He's pinched it from someone. The likes of him don't carry such an item. We found him lurking in the kitchen, eating the meat pie that was left. He sneaked into the house, is what he did, but he's wretched poor at it—noisy as a drunk man. A right dimwit." Willum lay still, apparently not choosing to say anything into the grass beneath his face.

"I believe you can let him up now, Larkin," St. Ives said to her, taking the watch and fob that she held out to him. "His name is Willum, and he and I are friends." Larkin stood up, as did Willum, who looked desperately unhappy. "Let me introduce you to Cleo and Eddie, Willum. They're my children. Your captor's name is Larkin." Willum said nothing, but hung his head.

"Is the timepiece yours, sir?" Larkin asked St. Ives.

"It's Mr. Pink's is what it is," Willum said.

"Mr. *Pink*," Larkin repeated. "Mr. Thingamabob, like as not."

"He tells the truth, Larkin," St. Ives said. And then to Willum, he said, "Is that why you ran when the constable came up?"

He nodded his head and looked at the ground. "I'd have been hung, else, like my old dad."

"They don't hang younkers any more," Larkin said. "That was quit a long time ago."

Willum shrugged and began to sniffle, covering his eyes with his hand. Cleo put her hand on his shoulder and told him not to cry, and Eddie told him that he was "among friends." Larkin said, "Leastways *you* won't hang. Not for foisting a watch."

"Did you follow me home?" St. Ives asked. "You must have."

"Aye. You stopped there in the wood, but I waited for you to go on. I don't..." He began to cry again, and Larkin rolled her eyes at the weakness. "I l-lost my *shillings*," he said, reaching into his pocket, and then fell to his knees and began searching the grass. Cleo and Eddie undertook to help him, but it was Larkin who found three of them, she having an eye for misplaced coins, although she wasn't particular about how they were misplaced. Willum found the missing fourth.

"You may keep the pocket-watch, Willum," St. Ives said, handing it back to him when he was on his feet again. "Mr. Pink won't be needing it, and I know for a fact that he owes you wages. But you must do us the service of speaking to Constable Brooke tomorrow morning. You remember what I said to you this afternoon?"

"About the man what burnt the village?"

"Just so. You and I will win our friend's freedom tomorrow. It's our good luck that you're among us now. You'll sleep in the company of Cleo, Eddie, and Larkin, the lot of you now being friends, although you and I must set out early in the morning."

"Burnt the village?" Larkin said. "*That's* a hanging offense, and no doubt about it."

"Not an *actual* village," St. Ives told her. He took Cleo, Eddie, and Larkin aside and said, "Willum mustn't be allowed to escape. He's our friend, as I said, and must be treated as such, but he's on parole. Do you follow me?"

"Don't fret, sir," Larkin said flatly. "He's safe as a baby with us."

Within the half hour—the four children having devoured the rest of the meat pie, half a loaf of bread, a wedge of cheese, and a quantity of Mrs. Langley's lemonade—St. Ives lay once again in his bed. He found that his happiness at recovering Willum had faded, and his mind was on Alice again. Hasbro's armed presence, along with two constables, was enough to keep her safe throughout the night. If Pink had cooked up the photographs and produced the broadsheet—and surely it was sensible to argue that he had—and if it were certain that he had been murdered by a mysterious third party and not by Bill

Kraken, then they would have taken a giant step toward bringing down the rickety evidence stacked against Alice and Mother Laswell. But there was no bringing it down until Willum had spoken to Constable Brooke.

He awakened before dawn from an uneasy sleep and hurriedly splashed water onto his face, combed his hair with his fingers, and dressed in the darkness. He arrived downstairs to discover from Mrs. Langley that Gilbert hadn't returned from Snodland. He had gone off last night to meet with Townover and his lawyers, with thoughts of overnighting at Windhover. Willum was asleep, although the other children were up and dressed, Mrs. Langley assuring St. Ives that all was well with them. She was wide-awake, she said, and they would put nothing over on her, not this morning, they wouldn't.

"I'll roust the boy," she said, and St. Ives nodded, discovering that he was in a desperate hurry to be away.

Chapter 20

Mother Laswell
in the Woods

A LONG THE VERY BACK of Hereafter
farm, beyond the ten-acre meadow that bounded
the rear of the property, a brook flowed through
the woods—Hampton Brook, a trout stream if there
were fishermen about—but a lonely stream and woods
for weeks on end where the silence was broken by the
wind in the trees, the calling of birds, and the rustle of
animals. There were chalk hills above the brook, the
chalk eroded over eons, rainwater percolating into the
hills themselves and hollowing out shallow caves.

Mother Laswell had slept in one such cave for two
nights running. Its entrance was hidden by shrubbery and
so was invisible from the path along the brook. Despite

the privacy and the quiet, however, her sleep had been uneasy, and to keep her mind from swerving, she had spent her waking hours doggedly considering the speech that she meant to deliver that very morning, come what may, to the Paper Dolls who assembled on the dock to take the ferry across to the mill. They were close to walking out—all signs pointed to it—and she meant to put her shoulder to the wheel.

She had hauled leaves and ferns into the cavern for a bed, and after a long night of it she was stiff and sore—very ready to pursue what might easily be her final bow. Bill was imprisoned for murder, she knew that much. If he had done what they said he had done, he had done it for her—foolishly, but out of love. She would have stopped him with a brickbat if she could have, but she couldn't. He had been gone before anyone knew what he was about. What was done was done. With any luck—if he wasn't hanged—they would be imprisoned together, away from the turmoil of the world. That was her final hope when she awakened this morning—to finish the job at hand and then to live out her days in a cell.

She hoisted herself wearily to her feet and dusted off her clothing, smoothing the wrinkled material as best she could, the flame-colored fabric dimmed by dust and stains. Dawn was some way off, but there was enough moonlight so that she could see it twinkling on the water of the brook. She descended the steep bank, holding thankfully onto branches until she was on level ground. The wet sand still held Hasbro's footprints. He had come along yesterday afternoon searching for her and had called her name several times. He was a fine, good man, and he hoped to help her, but she had business to attend to, and she meant to complete that business without any hindrance, no matter from whom.

She knelt on a flat rock, said a prayer, and washed her face and hands in the cold water of the brook before she drank from it. There was nothing for her to eat, but her appetite had quite disappeared when the police had come for her and told her what Bill had done and had found the trash that Townover's lackeys had hidden behind the barn. She looked back at the mouth of the cavern—what might prove to be her last home this side of prison—and she thought about Hereafter Farm: what joys it had given her over the years, and the interesting fact that she might soon be bound for another sort of hereafter, if the fiends undertook to treat her as they had treated poor Daisy. She had to assume they were searching for her.

Savoring the smell of the dewy vegetation and the cool dawn breeze, she walked away feeling lighter than she would have imagined. She skirted the meadow, keeping to the trees so as not to be seen in the moonlight, and made her way by a circuitous route toward the River Medway, listening to the symphony of birdsong in the awakening day, a music that was both beautiful and lonely.

Chapter 21

Into Snodland

N OTHING YET!" EDDIE SHOUTED in a hoarse whisper from his place in the high, loft window, where he was nearly invisible against the early morning darkness. His narrow landing looked out toward the house and the moonlit wisteria alley. Cleo stood beside him, gripping the fabric of his shirt. A long wooden ladder rose to the landing, where there was a swivel crane and a pulley for hauling objects up and in. It was also useful if a person wanted to make a quick descent, although it wasn't an approved caper, and the crane was most often swung inward and used for hoisting the heavy saddle onto the back of Johnson the elephant. Johnson had been saddled and ready to go out these last ten minutes.

Two lanterns were lit in the barn, one of them casting light on Johnson's enormous food box. Currently he was gobbling down the last vestiges of fruit, dried hops, sugar-canes, and two-day-old buns from the baker's. He drank greedily from his water trough when the food was gone, slopping the water around with his trunk for sheer sport, and then walked a distance before defecating enormously on a litter of straw.

"Willum has just come out," Eddie told them. "I'll watch for father."

Larkin and Finn, waiting by the barn door, waved up at him in acknowledgement. "Do you love Miss Alice, then?" Larkin asked Finn, who stood holding onto Johnson's tether. "It's plain in your face when she's about."

"Why do you say that?" Finn asked dismissively. "She's married to the Professor. I can't love her. It isn't honorable."

"You *liar*. You know what I mean. You're soft for her, Finn. She's a real lady. When I met her in London, she was good to me, even before she knew me, as was Uncle Gilbert, who took me in as his own. My old dad had been dead the past two years. I don't remember my mum."

"Do you miss that life along the river?" Finn asked. "I don't miss it."

She shrugged noncommittally and said, "Some. That's the past, though. I don't pay the past any heed. What I don't like is all this talk of witches."

"That's humbug," Finn said. "None of it's true."

"No one cares what's true. I heard tell of an old man in Essex who was a witch. They dragged him in the river to get the truth out of him. He died of it, and those that done it was let off. You've been around good people too long, Finn. You don't know enough of what people do to each other."

"I know more than you think, Larkin. I take your meaning, though. But Eddie and Cleo don't need to hear about witches being drowned."

"Mayhaps. I'm saying that if they killed this man Henry, who they say hanged himself, they'll treat Alice the same. Don't think they won't."

"I *know* they won't," Finn said, "because I won't let them."

"There it is, then," she said, staring at him. "That's what I've been saying." There was something unsettling in Larkin's face. It wasn't just pluck, although she had plenty of that, it was something more dangerous than pluck, and it surprised him coming from a girl as slight and young as Larkin.

"Here's father now! They're just climbing into the gig," Eddie said in a hoarse whisper. "They're off!" He started down the ladder, moving slowly, mindful of Cleo, who was following just a few rungs above him. Once they were on the floor they dashed to the barn door and ascended to the platform from which they climbed down onto Johnson's saddle.

"I'll drive Johnson," Larkin said, taking up the reins. "Boggs showed me how to drive a coach and four, and an elephant is much alike. Anyone can see that."

Finn agreed, given that he could hold the tether, and they stepped out of the barn. There was red along the eastern horizon, but it was still dark. They set out straightaway, but hadn't gone ten elephant steps toward the wisteria alley when Mrs. Langley stepped out of the house, walked in front of Dr. Johnson, and held up her hand. The elephant stopped dutifully and stood still.

"Don't for a moment think that I don't know what you're about," she said to the lot of them. "I overheard you plotting last night, but I thought it was play or I would have had the lot of you shackled to your beds. The Professor won't allow this kind of lark, which you very well know—sneaking out the moment he's vanished up the road. Back into the barn with you. Get Johnson settled and come in to breakfast."

Finn, much relieved, led the beast back the way they'd come, where Larkin, Cleo, and Eddie climbed down.

"I'll see to Johnson," Finn said, and he set about lifting the heavy saddle from the elephant's back with the crane. Eddie, Cleo, and Larkin trudged away. After ten minutes everything was secure, and Finn found himself alone, daylight pending in the east. He peered out past the barn door, and seeing no one out and about, he sprinted toward the road, crossed into the woods, and ran at an easy pace in the direction of the weir, where the water was shallow enough to ford. He was quickly across the stony path, his shoes dry, and moving down-river. Aylesford Village and the old bridge stood away to his left and behind him, the dawn light grey through the trees on his right hand.

He slowed to catch his breath, but after five minutes of brisk walking he heard the sound of running footsteps behind him, and he turned to see Larkin, coming up fast. He stopped until she caught up. He could see that she was angry for being left behind, and for a moment it looked as if she might mean to throttle him.

"It was you who peached to Mrs. Langley," she said. "She was watching out the window for us. I saw her plain. And I saw you bolt as soon as she was out of sight again."

"It was Cleo and Eddie I was thinking about. Like I told you, they shouldn't come along. They'd come to harm, and then what? But Eddie had to *think* he was com-ing along, do you see? He wouldn't stand for being left out, his own mother in jail and all. I knew you'd find a way."

"You'd best believe I'd find a way."

She looked into his face until he nodded, having noth-ing useful to say in reply, and then they set out again at a run, Larkin seeming to skim along over the ground without effort, as if she had done plenty of running in her life. In fifteen minutes they came out of the trees, the river before them, the road stretching away along it. They could see the ferry dock in the distance, people milling, black smoke rising from the chimney of the ferry. There was a gabble of noise on the wind coming up the river—a general shouting and confusion from the riverside in Snodland, and, as they stood trying to make out the extent of the trouble, the unmistakable sound of a rifle firing.

"How far to the bridge?" Larkin asked breathlessly.

"A mile and a half, more or less."

"And then down again. Three miles. We'll be too late."

Farther along the weedy shore a small dock stood with its pilings in the water, two rowing boats tied alongside, belonging, no doubt, to the farmhouses visible through the trees behind. The tide was just starting to turn, flowing slowly back toward the sea. Without a word Larkin hurried down the shore and leapt up onto the dock, where she untied the mooring line of a quick-looking boat with a sharp bow.

"We must return it," Finn said. "You know that, don't you?"

"Talk is a waste of time," she said. The two of them climbed in, and Larkin unshipped the oars, spun the boat like a whirligig, and looked back over her shoulder at the far shore as she slung them out into the river. The current helped to propelled them downstream, and very soon they were passing the first farms at the edge of the village of Snodland, people up and about, a man leading a pair of oxen along the road. Larkin heaved on the oars, the shore drawing closer, and Finn wondered just what they would do—whether an enemy would present itself, whether Larkin harbored a scheme in her mind, whether the Professor was nearby, or Hasbro...

He saw movement on shore now, a woman, heavy-set in a bright, orange-red dress, hurrying down out of the trees: Mother Laswell, heading for the river's edge above the tannery. She staggered forward rather than ran. Gravity seemed to be lending her momentum while threatening to dash her to the ground at every step.

Finn was thrown forward as the boat shot up onto the beach and stuck in the weedy sand. Larkin leapt out and Finn followed, hauling the boat up above the flood where it would be high and dry. Mother Laswell lumbered on some distance ahead, and by the time the boat was secure, she had disappeared into the crowd of girls crowding the road around the ferry landing, their voices rising into a loud chant.

Chapter 22

Testimony

——————

"WELL NOW," CONSTABLE BROOK said when St. Ives and Willum walked into the small office that fronted the one-cell jail where Bill Kraken was held. "I thought you were Dr. Pullman coming round. He sent to say that he's done with his examination of the baby. I expect him any moment now. Who is this boy, then?"

"This is my young friend Willum," St. Ives answered, and Willum tipped his cap as St. Ives had told him to do, then sank into his chair, his chin pressed against his chest. "Willum has news of the murder in Tunbridge Wells."

"Does he now? Has he heard of the reward that's been offered? The Benevolent Society has promised fifty pounds for information leading to the identity of the assailant, but it looks very much as if it's Bill, although it grieves me to say it. This is something new, then?"

"Yes," St. Ives told him. "It's plain fact, I believe—fact that will show that Bill Kraken is innocent of the crime. Speak your piece Willum."

"You needn't be afraid." Brooke told him, when he saw the boy's hesitation, and he opened a drawer in his desk and drew out a parchment package. "Do you fancy a piece of Blackpool Rock, perhaps?" Without waiting for an answer he removed a stick of rock from its wrapper and cracked it against the edge of the desk, handing a big piece to Willum, who snatched it up, closed his hand around it, and thrust his hand between his knees.

Willum looked around furtively, and perhaps seeing that there was no escape, he said. "I seen Pink die. The man scragged him. Here." He thumped his chest with the hand holding the piece of sugar rock as if it were a knife.

"You saw this, with your own eyes?" Brooke said.

Willum nodded. "I worked for Pink. Leastways sometimes. I was there in the old barn, and I saw it plain through the window."

"The tumbledown shanty behind, do you mean?"

"Aye, sir. Pink gave me the odd shilling and said I could sleep dry if I was to sleep there."

"And this man who scragged Pink, how do you know he wasn't the same fellow who sits in my very jail?"

"I seen your man, sir. A tall man. Narrow. His hair stuck up from his head and his ears like…" He held his open hands to his ears by way of illustration. "He wore red gaiters and his pants had a stripe to them, and a patch on the back as had been sewed on."

"That's right. I see that you're a truthful boy. What did you see him do?"

"Well, sir…" Willum started, and he told the story just as he'd told it to St. Ives, about how Kraken had gone into Pink's through the back door, and then Pink had come out in a hurry and met his fate, stabbed in the chest by a burly sort of a man, whose face was hidden by a hood. "He weren't much taller than Mr. Pink, but terrible strong, like my dad, who carried hod. Old Pink went over onto his back, and the man hauled him to his feet like nothing. Pink turned to run, the blood running out, but the man pushed him up the steps, opened the door, and flung him in. Then he run off, the man did."

Brooke sat back in his chair and considered this for a moment. "Bill Kraken tells the same story, Professor. It made no difference, of course, when it was just Bill himself telling it. Until someone else tells the same story, it isn't worth a farthing. Kraken says that Pink struck him over the head with a glass paperweight, which explains the wound. But why would Pink have done so if Kraken hadn't attacked him?"

"It's as I told you," St. Ives said, "the photographs of the so-called witches were clever fabrications. Pink contrived them in his laboratory using the photographs that he took at Mother Laswell's soirée. Something had gone wrong for him, though. His employers wished to silence him, or so I believe, and Bill caught him in the act of running."

"What of the dead baby, then? Surely Pink wasn't a ghoul who would kill a baby."

"I don't dispute that there was a dead baby, although the entire business is highly suspicious. Pink was of course paid to manufacture evidence."

There was the sound of a wagon drawing up outside. "Here's Dr. Pullman just now arriving," Brooke said. "I'll ask the pertinent questions, if you don't mind, Professor."

In a moment the door opened and Dr. Pullman entered, wearing a stained doctor's smock, a cold pipe in his mouth. There were greetings, and Pullman sat in the remaining chair. "The long and short of it is that the baby was stillborn," he told them. "It never drew an earthly breath. They're easy enough to acquire, you know. There's a class of midwives that earn pin money selling them. In short, there is no *murdered* baby, only the corpse of a baby never born."

"What of the bloody wound, then?" Brooke asked.

"The blood was that of pig, probably, although any animal would do. If the blood had been fresh, I could have been more certain that it wasn't human blood, but the cells contract and shrivel as they dry, and it becomes quite impossible to distinguish human blood from animal blood. In any event, dead things do not bleed. The blood, as I say, was a theatrical addition."

"I see." Brooke looked out through the window. A breeze had come up, and a gust blew a flurry of leaves past. "Give me a moment, please, gentlemen." He went out, and after a moment returned, ushering a haggard Bill Kraken along before him.

"That's the man!" Willum said, sitting up straight in his chair and pointing.

"You're certain," Constable Brooke asked him. "It's not just the red gaiters and the trousers? Any man can wear such an outfit, you know."

"No, sir. That's the man as went into Pink's, but not the man what put the knife into him."

"Bill," St. Ives said, standing up to shake his friend's hand, "this is Willum, who saw Manfred Pink murdered in Tunbridge Wells. He's offered up testimony that's set you free."

"And he's earned himself fifty pounds from the Benevolent Society into the bargain," Brooke added, smiling at Willum now.

Kraken stared at the boy for a moment and then began to weep. "They called *me* Willum when I was a lad," he said, "and now this." He wiped his eyes. "It's the mouths of babes, is what it is, like the Testament tells us. It was ever so. What word of Mother, Professor? I fear for her."

"No word," St. Ives said. "She took to the woods, apparently, and as far as I know she's still hiding. I intend to carry the news into Snodland immediately, however. The sooner we clear away the hokum, the safer our wives will be."

Chapter 23

The Mob

ALICE STOOD ON THE iron frame of her cot, watching the sunrise through the barred window, great slashes of red and orange against a blue-black sky that was lightening by the moment. She had a downhill view to the river, and could see the ferry dock in the near distance, and she heard the voices of several girls, Paper Dolls coming down from their dormitory. The world was waking up, and she was happy to see daylight at last.

She didn't dare show herself in the window, but stood well to the side in order to avoid the rocks pitched through the bars from across the road. A mob had congregated two hours ago, carrying torches. They'd been quiet at first, but then in a body had commenced to chant, "Witch!"

and "Hell spawn!" and other epithets. To Alice's ear there was a theatrical quality about it, although the stones and rotten fruit thrown at the window hadn't been theatrical in the least, and still lay scattered and splattered on the floor of her cell. Hasbro had fastened the shutters over the windows, which stopped the pelting. He and the night constable, Reginald Fisk, stood between her and the mob.

She had listened to the sound of the two men exhorting the crowd to go home, Fisk threatening them with the Riot Act. Quiet had ensued for a time shortly before dawn. Fisk had retired when another constable, a large, hairy, uncouth man named Bates, had spelled him. Shortly thereafter, Bates had sent Hasbro away for two hour's sleep, assuring him that he would keep the peace.

But then, inexplicably the shutters had come off the jail window and the mob had worked itself up again. Constable Bates had apparently gone away—had left Alice without a guard. At best it was unlikely behavior for a constable. At worst… She wondered how Bill Henry had managed to hang himself. There was nothing but the bars on the windows to support a man's weight. He'd perhaps leapt from the cot, although it would have meant a very short noose and a very small man. Had the oaf Bates helped Bill Henry die…?

Alice chanced a look at the mob—a score of people now, including two men leading a heavy mule and carrying an ominous coil of rope tied to a three-pronged grapnel. They hadn't the appearance of villagers—not more than two or three shabby women and the rest mean looking men probably hired out of pubs. The full weight of this bore down upon her, and she wondered where Langdon was, and Gilbert, and the rest of her friends. She looked around for a weapon of some sort, but her iron cot was too stoutly built to dismantle.

Gilbert's largesse had furnished the room with a wash-stand built of oak, however, with three turned legs, and after only a moment's hesitation, she darted across to it, crouching so as to be out of sight of the window, and removed the pitcher and basin. She picked up the table, held on tightly to two of the legs, and slammed it against the wall until it broke apart, leaving her with two unbroken legs. She hefted one of them and wondered whether Constable Bates would appear outside the cell door to see about the noise she'd made. But the moments passed and there was no Bates. She shouted his name, but still there was no response. Apparently she'd been abandoned altogether.

A man's voice arose in anger beyond the window now, and she hazarded another glance outside, where she saw none other than Charles Townover himself astride a bay horse, haranguing the mob, which jeered at him heartily, two or three persons pelting him with eggs and stones.

He shook his fist, received a derisive howl, and then gave off and trotted away toward the river. Alice considered this. If the mob were hired either to frighten her or assault her, it would have been Townover who had done the hiring. But clearly that was not the case.

What on earth *was* the case? She looked down toward the ferry dock, beyond which black smoke arose from the ferry's chimney, the boat itself sitting idle. The road in front of the platform was filling with Paper Dolls standing in a mass, blocking Townover's way. As if on cue they took up a chant, "Strike! Strike! Strike!" Townover's horse, perhaps spooked by the noise, shied sideways, and Townover lost his top-hat, the chanting momentarily replaced by laughter.

Now someone was ascending to the platform—a woman in a voluminous, flaming dress, back-lit by the rising sun. Her wild hair glowed like a golden aura around her head, and she held up both hands as if granting a blessing, and then began to shout.

God help us, Alice thought. It was Mother Laswell, come to throw an iron plow into the works of the Majestic Paper Mill just as she had threatened. Charles Townover hollered something in response, waving one arm over his head, but a vast cheering arose and drowned him out. When the cheering faded, Mother Laswell began to magnify her exhortations through cupped hands, and the crowd fell silent. Even the mob across the road was listening. "The murderers you work for," she shouted, "have stolen your health and your…"

But now there was a hue and cry from the mob, as if time was wasting, and Alice heard the sounds of running feet and struggle. She looked out and saw that Hasbro had returned, thank God, his rifle pointed into the air. Fisk was there also with a truncheon. There was the crack of the rifle, and the mob fell back. But they hadn't lost their spirit, for they rushed forward in a mass now, knocking Hasbro to the ground, a man wrenching at his rifle, Hasbro using a man's weight to pull himself to his knees.

There were hands on the bars of the window, and Alice swung her club, smashing fingers, blood squirting from split knuckles. A bruiser with a hammered face slipped the grapnel through the bars and pulled it tight, two of the prongs catching hold. Alice thrust her table-leg through the bars, hitting the man in the forehead, but he wrenched her club from her hand, cursing into her face. She pried at the grapnel, trying to twist it loose, but the rope was taut—tied to a yoke around the neck of the mule, which surged forward, two men beating it on the flanks. Brick dust squirted from the mortar in the joints of the wall.

Alice picked up the remaining chair leg, which seemed like a frail sort of war club now, and watched through the window as Constable Fisk swung his truncheon in the midst of the melee until he was borne down and trampled underfoot. Hasbro was up again by now, knocking people's heads with the butt of his rifle, his back against a tree. A man grabbed Hasbro's collar from behind and wrenched him aside, tripping him up, and now Alice could see neither Hasbro nor Fisk from where she stood, just the grunting and shouting mob and the mule straining forward.

She looked down toward the ferry dock, where Townover sat futilely at the edge of the throng, Mother Laswell shouting stridently, her hands gesturing. And then, uncannily, from out of the throng of Paper Dolls, Larkin appeared, shouldering her way through and running hard up the road, Finn Conrad at her heels.

Alice found her voice and hollered uselessly at Larkin to cease, but the girl ran into the midst of the riot and sprang ape-like upon the back of the man who was harassing Hasbro, grabbed fistfuls of the man's hair in both hands, and with a wild cry clamped her teeth onto on the man's ear. He reeled away, caroming off the flanks of the straining mule just as the bars of the cell window were yanked outward in an avalanche of bricks.

Through the breach in the wall Alice caught a brief glimpse of the top of the road—a cart swinging into view, coming down at a breakneck pace, Constable Brook driving the two horses. Langdon sat alongside, holding onto the wagon with one hand and his hat with the other, and Bill Kraken rode in the back, a death-or-glory look on his face.

Alice let out a whoop of joy. Sheltered by the remains of the wall, she set her feet and held her club over her shoulder, swinging it hard at the first man near enough, hitting him solidly above the eye. A hail of stones flew through the breach in the wall, and she was forced to back away. She heard a boy's voice—Finn's voice—directly behind her, shouting, "Miss Alice!"

The cell door was swinging open, Finn hauling on it. She leapt through, turning and throwing her weight against it as it clanged shut, Finn turning an iron key in the lock. Two men slammed hard against the door, shouting curses, and Alice banged one of them in the neck for good measure before dashing after Finn down the short hallway and out into the open air, Finn grabbing her hand and leading her down the narrow street toward the river. Two men and a woman ran past them, members of the manufactured mob, obviously getting out while the getting was good.

She realized that she still held onto her table leg, but she had no desire to club anyone with it. The thought came into her mind to keep it as a trophy, but in the light of day she saw that the end of it was bloody, and she pitched it away. Mother Laswell stood in silence with the assembled girls on the ferry landing now, and it was quiet along the river, the prevailing noise being the chugging of the steam engine on the ferry, which was heading for the opposite bank. Charles Townover sat astride his horse on deck, his head bowed.

Chapter 24

Two Bottles of Chemical

I T WAS EARLY IN the morning, the sun just up, Clover and Henley having made a long night of it. Henley sat at the desk in the office with a disheveled Clover on his lap. Her bodice was pulled down, and Henley's undergarments were awry. A half-empty wine bottle sat on the desk, and two more lay on the carpet. When Charles Townover walked in through the door, hatless and his coat filthy, his cane knocking against the floorboards, he stopped dead and stared for a long moment at the two revelers, who stared straight back at him. He took in the shambles of the office and the empty bottles and nodded slowly.

"You've been celebrating, I see," he said in a shaky voice. "May I ask what it is that generated this revelry, given that the Paper Dolls have walked out on strike?"

Clover slowly pulled up her bodice, but then sat very still, her hands in her lap, waiting for Henley to break the deadly silence.

"We're celebrating mortality," he said, leering at his father. "Your own mortality in particular."

Townover glared back at him, his face petrified with rage. And then in a wild burst he turned to Clover and shrieked, "Harlot!" and bounded forward, raising his cane as if to strike her and kicking the desk with his boot.

Clover leapt to her feet, tottering backwards as Townover brought the cane hissing downward. Henley reached up and caught it with his hand, yanking it free and flinging it back over his shoulder. Townover nearly fell, but he caught himself on the desk. He was shaking now, a full-bodied shaking, as if overcome with an irresistible palsy.

Clover stared at him in surprise and then began to laugh, puffing out her chest like a pigeon and said, "You *like* what you see, don't you, you wicked old man."

Henley, having arranged his undergarments, sat silently in the chair. His eyes were active, however, as if he were coming to a conclusion.

"This is *infamous*," Townover said to him in a hoarse whisper. And then, "Get out, you leering whore!" he shouted, turning on Clover again "Get *out*, I say." And he stamped his foot, although the gesture was frail and impotent.

"Stay!" Henley commanded, and Clover stood her ground, favoring Townover with theatrically lascivious glances.

"What of the fat man?" Henley asked.

"If you mean Gilbert Frobisher," Townover said in what was meant as a thundering voice, "he has made a handsome investment in the mill, and I've granted him a position of some importance. You'll answer to him from this moment on, if, indeed, you answer to anyone at all."

"I choose to answer to myself and myself alone, sir."

Clover moved behind Henley, putting the desk between herself and Townover. The old man's palsy had subsided, but his chest was heaving with the exertion of his anger, and his face was scarlet, completely suffused with blood, his breath wheezing out of his throat. Winking at him, Clover picked up the wine bottle and drank from it, setting it down again onto the corner of the desk and then belching loudly.

Townover gasped out a hoarse breath, seemed to choke on it, and reeled sideways, losing his balance and falling to one knee. He reached into his coat, shakily removing his flask of nitroglycerine elixir and fumbling with the cap. The task of opening it was apparently beyond his powers.

"Let me help you, father," Henley said, in a voice of mock concern, and he stood up and went to his father's side, taking the bottle from his hand, loosening the stopper and purposely dumping the liquid up and down the leg of his father's trousers. "Good *heavens*," he said. "How *clumsy* of me."

Townover, a look of horror on his face, bent forward and began to suck the elixir from his pant-leg. He clutched his chest, and a croaking noise stuttered from his throat.

"Fetch the bottle of chemical in the bottom drawer Clover, and the folded cloth along with it," Henry said briskly. "It'll settle him." He knelt on the floor in his stocking feet, supporting his father's back.

Clover handed him the heavy bottle and the folded cloth, watching as he thumbed out the glass stopper and poured out a stream of chemical, the sweet reek of chloroform rising around them, smelling something like wine and rot. Henley pressed the sopping rag to his father's face, encircling the old man's chest with his free arm, and bore down on his back embracing him tightly. His father flapped his arms feebly and made sounds in his chest, as if trying to speak. Very slowly, however, the struggling stopped. Henley remained kneeling, his head bowed, the rag still pressed to his father's face.

It was borne in upon Clover that the old man was dead, and that her own fate hung in the balance. She found that she could scarcely breathe. She'd be hung. She wouldn't live long enough to be hanged... She slid her hand into the open drawer and drew out the wallet of money that had been hidden by the cloth and bottle. She tucked it into her bodice, looking at Henley's bowed form and hoping to God that he was too far removed to wonder what she was about. She glanced at the door, bile rising into her throat. If she ran, he would surely catch her.

Henley pitched the saturated cloth aside now, finally, turning his head upward as if to breathe in clean air, and then he put the glass stopper back into the bottle, leaving it on the floor. He looked again at the ceiling for a long, silent moment, nodded as if with satisfaction, and turned to speak. "My father's heart seems to have given out, alas. Find Mr. Davis, who should be up and about in his quarters by now. Tell him to send for the doctor. And on the way, throw this bottle and rag into the privy. Pour out the contents and drop the bottle in after it."

"Yes, sir," Clover said, and, careful of the wallet, she quickly donned her slippers and picked up the bottle, taking the rag by a dry corner. She hurried out through the door, and once out of sight she took the stairs downward two at a time, hiking up her dress and heading through the side door to the row of privies along the brook, with their stinking pits and buckets of slaked lime. Immediately she saw Davis himself—the back of him, stepping into a privy—and she pulled back into the mill doorway until the privy door was shut.

She stepped out again, moving quickly but quietly. She eased open the door to the first privy in line, dropped the rag into the swill at the bottom, and poured out the chemical. She followed it with the bottle before darting out again and back into the mill, where she watched once again from behind the edge of the door, waiting for Davis to come out.

"Mr. Davis!" she shouted when he did so. "Thank God!"

"What's amiss, girl?" he asked, hitching up his trousers.

"It's old Mr. Townover," she gasped out. "Upstairs. His heart has burst. I'm to run for the doctor. Mr. Henley asked me to summon you." With that she dashed away along the brook, fully expecting to be run down and captured. But when she looked back Davis was nowhere to be seen—he had gone in, thank Christ. The ruse might lend only a few moments, however, before he understood that she had fled, and would come for her.

Her mind turned as she ran on. She remembered what Henley had said to her—that the bottled chemical in his drawer quietened the girls when they were frightened. Had Daisy been a frightened girl? *Were there others?* She thought of Letty Benton, who had lived with her and Daisy at the Chequers and had 'gone into London' and hadn't returned.

Abruptly she turned off the path and into the woods, heading in the general direction of the Snodland Bridge, where she might cross if only she could hurry. She thought of her trunk with the pitiful coins she had stolen from her aunt tucked beneath the fabric in the bottom. The lot of it was nothing but rubbish for a girl with a purse of money tucked into her bodice. She began to run again, but straight toward the river now through the trees. Never in her life had she had this much to lose. There was no time for the bridge. She soon broke from the woods below where Eccles Brook emptied into the Medway, and there, two hundred yards down the bank, the ferry stood empty at the dock.

Across the way in Snodland the Paper Dolls were milling in the street, and there was the sound of shouting and cheering. It was the strike, and she laughed out loud, almost wishing she could join them, for she hated Henley and Davis and even old man Townover despite his being dead—good hate wasted, it seemed to her. She hurried out onto the dock and stepped aboard the ferry.

"Mr. Townover must have a doctor immediately," she said to the pilot. He took in the look on her face, cast off the lines, and headed out across the river.

Chapter 25

She Might Be in Hell

HENLEY HAD PULLED HIS collective parts together and was sitting placidly at his desk, waiting for Davis to arrive. He contemplated the events of the morning, which had not fallen out quite as he had expected. But the deed was done, and done conveniently. The bottle and the rag were down the privy, so to say. (Clover would have done as he had asked, failing at her own peril.) There would surely be no autopsy, given the state of the old man's heart. Henley would tear up the agreement with Gilbert Frobisher. Windhover and the mill would belong to him. It had turned out to be a profitable morning all the way around. Davis was the only porcupine left in the path.

And now Davis appeared at the top of the stairs, threw the door open, and strode in. He saw Townover's dead body on the floor. He sniffed at the reek of chloroform on the air. He squinted at Henley. But Henley cared nothing for Davis's opinion of things. One didn't ask for permission to murder one's own father. The center drawer of the desk was slid partway open, and Charles Townover's Lancaster pistol lay inside—a .577 calibre howdah pistol he had brought back from India many years ago. The bullet was meant to stop lions, and certainly it would put an end to Davis.

"Where is Clover?" Henley asked.

"She told me you'd sent her for the doctor. But she might be in hell, for all I care. So you've murdered him? You took it upon yourself to murder him?"

"He had an apoplectic fit and dropped dead—the best of all possible outcomes."

"If they cut him open, they'll find the chloroform in him. His innards will be blue. You know that. Where's the bottle?"

"Why would they cut open a man whose heart is known to be worthless? The bottle is gone, along with the cloth; that's enough. The reek will fade. There will be no evidence, and I, of course, will be desolated by my poor father's death. So, one thing at a time, did you ask Jenks about Pink's money?"

"Aye, he denied taking it, which was a bare-faced lie, so I shot him and dumped his body into the marsh. But that's nothing. You've put my head in the gallows, and your own, too, murdering the old man. Do you think that Clover won't rat?"

"Clover, do you say? She's neck deep in all of this, and she has a criminal past. She'd scarcely go to the police. You needn't fear Clover."

"I don't fear any woman," he said evenly, "nor any man."

Henley reached into the drawer and withdrew the pistol, which he pointed at Davis's midsection—not six feet away. "Then allow me to acquaint you with a truly fearful object. I don't quite trust you at the moment. You're lying to me, of course. Jenks had the money with him, as was true of Pink. And now you've got it. I'm a generous man, however. Keep it and walk away. Now."

Davis stared at him. "You paid Bates as much to throttle Bill Henry, or near to as much. It was me who set it up, and me who took the blows when we bearded Henry in the alley, as well as the rest of it: the evidence at the farm, the dead baby. It was me who made this work, not you. Bates still has his position, but I'm told to get the hell out. And I'll do it. I'll go. But I'll take the money in the drawer along with me. It's nothing to you now. You're rich. The money was laid by in case we had to bolt, or so you said, but it's me who'll bolt, not for the likes of you. We both gain if you do the right thing by me."

Henley watched for a moment, shrugged, and still pointing the pistol at Davis, used his left hand to slide the side drawer open. It took only a few seconds to discern that it was empty: the wallet was gone. He laughed out loud. "Miss Clover Cantwell has made fools of the both of us. She's taken the money and run. You can look if you like. Look into all the drawers."

"God *damn!*" Davis said, his face a mask of anger now.

"Wait," Henley said. He sat for a long moment as if thinking things through. "I sent her across the river to fetch the doctor, like you said. You can follow her track easily, and there'll be people on this side of the river or the other who have seen her. Here's what I say: bring her head to me, and I'll pay you another thousand pounds— money I have laid by, as you put it. Both of us will be free of her. Whatever Clover is carrying on her person is yours. Her person itself is yours, for that matter." He lowered the pistol now, and slid his hand back into the drawer as if to put it away.

Davis hesitated for a moment, mastering his temper. "I'll be back," he said, "with or without the girl." As he turned to go, Henley drew the pistol out of the drawer again and shot him between the shoulder blades.

Chapter 26

Clover's Confession

S T. IVES WALKED ALONE along the High Street, which was comparatively quiet. The Paper Dolls, finding themselves suddenly on holiday, were dispersing. Brooke and Hasbro had set out after the villain Bates, and Bill Kraken sat with Mother Laswell, Alice, Larkin, and Willum, waiting for St. Ives to have finished talking to Constable Fisk, the two of them putting the idiotic witch accusations to rest. There was still a villain to uncover, but surely that would come.

A girl approached him along the pavement now, hurrying along and looking down at the ground. It took him a moment to recognize her. She glanced up and apparently recognized him, also, for she ducked away down the alley behind the Malden Arms. *Clover*—that was

her name. St. Ives followed her into the alley. He had
gone into this same alley only a couple of days back, and
knew there was no outlet from the small yard that boxed
it in. As he rounded the near corner, she was standing
like a frightened child with nowhere to run except into
the rear door of the Malden Arms. He cut her off when
she bolted for it, however, and grabbed her wrist, stopping her flight.

"Clover Cantwell, I believe," he said, recalling her
full name, if in fact it was her name at all. "It's time for
the truth, girl. I'm giving you the opportunity to save
yourself."

"Let me go, sir. I won't run."

He did as he was asked, and she turned toward him,
her face full of tears and regret—alligator tears, perhaps, but it was unfair to assume such a thing. "Come,"
he said. "It's time for the truth. We know about Henley
Townover. You'd be a fool to lie for him." He was sensible of his own lie, Henley Townover's involvement
being a strong suspicion and nothing else. For good
measure he said, "The constable took him into custody
this morning."

"No, sir, he did not," she said "I left him not half an
hour past, and I'll tell you that he murdered his own
father with chemical. The bottle's down the privy. He
had his way with me sir, he threatened…"

She began to weep aloud now, and St. Ives recalled her arrival at Hereafter Farms, presenting the lot of them with the broadsheet, carrying the sham off like a born devil. Still, Henley Townover no doubt held sway over her.

"He threatened to murder my Aunt Gower in Maidstone. Worse than that, sir, but I can't say what I mean. It's too shameful. You don't know him, sir, nor did his own poor father. Mr. Townover's heart quit with the sorrow of it, although Henley helped it along. And now I'll hang for it—for wanting to help my poor Aunt Gower, who never hurt nobody in her life, and looks to me to care for her."

It seemed to St. Ives that the girl might well be telling the truth—some variety of truth anyway. Certainly her testimony would damn Henley Townover. "Will you make a full confession?" he asked.

"Yes, sir. If you write it out plain, I'll sign it. But you must put in that it was Henley that forced my hand. He had poor Daisy murdered, do you see, and I was to be next."

"We'll put it all in," St. Ives said, "Never you fear. Come along."

They walked together into the Malden Arms, where the publican was stirring a great black pot of beans on the stove-top. He was evidently surprised to see the two of them coming in from the back, but he fell into line when he recognized St. Ives and saw that Clover was weeping. He was happy enough to fetch St. Ives a pen, ink, and paper and stood by while Clover told her story: how Henley had chosen her from the lot of Paper Dolls, and had offered her money for Aunt Gower, and told her just what would happen to her and to her aunt if they didn't play along, and the grand life they would have if they did. Clover had hated it from the first moment, but dared not refuse his demands. She told them how she had overheard him tell Davis to have Mr. Pink murdered and how Davis himself took what they called "the evidence" to Hereafter Farm, the two of them laughing when they dreamed up the scheme. It was true that she did as she was told—what choice had she?—but it was also true that this morning she had fled when she had seen her chance. She had watched helplessly while Henley had poured out his father's medicine, and after the murder she had put the chloroform down the privy—the first in the line—just as she was told, the evidence there in the muck, and then had run away with nothing but the clothes on her back. She dared not go back to the Chequers for her possessions, because Davis would be waiting, and would take her to her death as he had taken Daisy Dumpel.

"And that's complete, then?" St. Ives asked at last.

"Yes, sir. There's no doubt more that they did, but they didn't tell me of it, as you can imagine. They used that bottle of chemical on the girls, I think. They must have. And they would have used it on me this very day."

She signed the document, a page and a half closely written. The publican signed as a witness. Clover began to weep again. "When I was in London," she said to St. Ives, "I was taken up for theft. I've a black mark against me, and it's justified. I don't like to say it, but it's true. I came to Maidstone to live with my Aunt Gower, and was hired at the mill, where I hoped to make my step and advance, as they say. It's all gone to smash now. All of it. Aunt Gower is barmy, and can't speak on my behalf. It'll be Colney Hatch for her and the jail for me. A confession is nothing to a judge. You know that, sir."

"There is some truth in what you say, Clover."

"More than some. I'll be bold, sir. I'll take my oath that all I want in life is another job such as the one that Henley Townover gave me and then took away again. It's nothing but a ruin now."

"I'm not convinced that anything is ruined. My good friend has bought shares in the mill, do you see, and there's no need to suppose that it's closing its doors. I'll vouch for you before the judge."

"*Will* you sir?" She lunged toward him now and, momentarily confused, gripped his arm and looked into his face. She turned away blushing and said, "I'm ashamed to ask it, sir, but I have three shillings to my name, and surely there'll be no work at the mill for a time. Can you give me the loan of two pound for my Aunt Gower and me to see us through? You're a good man, sir, and the only friend we have."

"No, girl," the publican said, reaching into his pocket. "You've a friend in me. Here's two quid, and give my best to your Aunt Gower. If you're down this way, I'll feed the both of you." He wiped a tear from his eye and turned away to his bean pot. St. Ives found a five-pound note in his own pocket and gave it to her, although not without misgivings. Still and all, if he refused her, his own soul was quite possibly damned. The worst that could come of being generous was that she would spend it, but then someone else would gain.

The two men watched her dart out the door. She would run, of course, Aunt Gower or no Aunt Gower, but at the moment that meant nothing to St. Ives. It occurred to him as he was walking back up the road to deliver the confession to Fisk, that he might give strong consideration to what he would tell Alice, who often accused him of sentimental gallantry.

Chapter 27

The Moral Question

S T. IVES FOUND HIS home and his bed a haven once again, but now it had been scoured of unclean spirits, and the course of early summer had steadied, the rocks and the shoal water behind them. "Tell me about this morning," he said to Alice, "now that we've finally got a moment of peace."

"I can tell you that when I cleaned the blood from Larkin's face she clung to me as if I were her mother," Alice said to St. Ives. "It put me out of sorts, despite the fact that her bloody mouth, or at least her teeth, had been tearing off a man's ear. I believe she's been raised by tigers."

"Gilbert tells me that she quite admires you—more than admires you. You have that same effect on Finn and of course on Eddie and Cleo. Children are notoriously good judges of character, you know. But you had started to tell me what had happened along the river. You mentioned a derelict boat."

"Well," she said, "it was an odd thing. The lot of us were sitting on that bit of meadow upwind from the tannery shortly before you arrived, eating a basket of food put up by the publican at the Malden Arms. A girl hurried out of the trees some distance upriver, where a rowing boat was drawn up onto the shore. I took little notice, but Larkin sprang up and stated that the girl meant to steal their boat."

"*Their* boat?" St. Ives asked, fixing the bed pillows behind him. "Larkin has no boat."

"Larkin and Finn had *borrowed* the derelict boat, it turned out, in order to cross the river on the way to rescuing me from prison. They meant to return it on the way home."

"Ah," St. Ives said, "a *borrowed* boat rather than a stolen boat. We can put the moral question to Vicar Hampson when we see him. It's beyond my powers." There was the sound of rain and wind from outside, and from time to time he heard small voices from downstairs, where the children were allegedly sleeping. He wondered how they found so much to say to each other.

"I've chosen to ignore the moral question altogether," Alice told him, although if we can discover the boat's owner we should compensate him. But as to what happened next, it was Mother Laswell who saw that the girl was none other than Clover Cantwell, and as soon as she mentioned the name, Bill leapt up with a wild look on his face and would have taken off at a run if Mother hadn't held onto his gaiters like a terrier. Clover was knee-deep in the river by now, climbing into the boat, and the tide was falling.

"Larkin was in a fit of pique, and she offered to borrow a second boat so that she and Finn could bring Clover to justice. Although I have a high regard for Larkin's powers, I decided to disallow it, and Mother agreed. Both of us were done up, and Larkin, of course, must not be provoked. As for Clover, she contrived to disappear beneath the thwarts, lying down on the deck, and by the time she passed the ferry dock she was far out on the river and the boat appeared to be empty."

"She had no idea that Davis was dead," St. Ives said, "and she was in fear of being caught—far more fear of Davis than of the police. She assumed that purchasing a rail or coach ticket might well be deadly. It seems somehow fitting that we provided the boat for her escape."

"I don't know that it's *fitting*, although I take your meaning."

St. Ives considered the five-pound note that he had given Clover in the name of her Aunt Gower—money that had gone downriver rather than up. Perhaps he would not mention it to Alice at all.

"Should I have told Constable Brooke about Clover's flight?" Alice asked.

"Surely you do not want the poor girl pursued."

"In what sense is Clover a 'poor girl,' Langdon?"

"She's been looking after her dowager aunt in Maidstone, working in those conditions at the mill." He shrugged, as if he had made his point.

"And doing the bidding of a man so wicked that air would scarcely allow itself to occupy his lungs."

"Her signed testimony attests to that. She gave me the evidence willingly. It was the completest thing—all mysteries solved."

"Her testimony was her alternative to being hanged. Tell me. Did you believe her tattle or did you merely feel sorry for the girl?"

St. Ives looked up at the tapestry and considered this. The spray of candle-lit stars looked back down upon him like so many eyes. "Some of both. It seemed to me that the world had cheated her. I have no idea of the extent of her guilt or innocence, but I'm certain that Henley Townover would have murdered her as he had the others—four bodies so far, and Pink into the bargain. Davis I don't count, for the man was as evil as his master, and we've no idea what happened to Jenks, who might have fled after murdering Pink. Henley Townover will hang, and no one will mourn his disappearance out of the world. So you see, I don't much mind that Clover out-ran her fate, and I have an aversion to women being put to death."

"Women but not men?"

"Yes, on the whole, although perhaps it doesn't stand to reason. I'll put it on the list of questions to ask the Vicar."

"Good enough." She looked at him for a long moment, and then said, "I'm happy that you're a deeply sentimental man, Langdon, but I wouldn't want to think that Clover Cantwell outwitted you."

"Outwitted me?" St. Ives said. "Not for a moment."